DATE DUE

AUG 3 1998			

SELECTED BY THE

JUNIOR LIBRARY CLUB

1998

Sparrows in the Scullery

Books by Barbara Brooks Wallace

Peppermints in the Parlor

The Barrel in the Basement

Perfect Acres, Inc.

The Twin in the Tavern

Cousins in the Castle

Sparrows in the Scullery

Barbara Brooks Wallace

Sparrows in the Scullery

A Jean Karl Book

✳

ATHENEUM BOOKS *for* YOUNG READERS

Atheneum Books for Young Readers
An imprint of Simon & Schuster Children's Publishing Division
1230 Avenue of the Americas
New York, New York 10020

Book design by Michael Nelson
The text of this book is set in Bembo.

First Edition
Printed in the United States of America
10 9 8 7 6 5 4 3 2 1

Library of Congress Cataloging-in-Publication Data
Wallace, Barbara Brooks.
Sparrows in the scullery / Barbara Brooks Wallace.—1st ed.
p. cm.
"A Jean Karl book."
Summary: Despite horrible conditions at the boys' home where
kidnappers have left him, eleven-year-old Colley, an orphan, finds
a reason and a way to live, along with comradeship.
ISBN 0-689-81585-9
[1. Orphans—Fiction. 2. Kidnapping—Fiction. 3. Friendship—Fiction.] I. Title.
PZ7.W1547Sp   1997
[Fic]—dc21
96-50916

*For my very own family—Jim, Jimmy, Christina, Victoria,
and Elizabeth—their very own book, with love*

Contents

Chapter I

Colley Trevelyan

With covers drawn tightly up around his chin, Colley lay rigid in his bed, trying to pay no attention each time a fierce gust of March wind moaned around the corners of the house, rattling the bare skeleton branches of the great oak tree outside his bedroom. All the while he kept his face carefully turned away from the three tall windows he felt were glaring at him with their cold, glassy eyes. Beyond the windows was only a deep and terrible darkness, unrelieved by a single tiny flickering pinprick of light from the gas lamps that ordinarily lit the wide circular driveway leading to the front door. They had either been forgotten or, for some reason, deliberately left unlit. Nothing, it seemed, was ever going to be the way it was before. Nothing!

Ordinarily, Cark, the butler, would have drawn the draperies against the night earlier in the evening. Then the heavy blue velvet would have muffled the sound of the wind and hidden the windows that became so frightening at night. But Cark was gone along with most of the rest of the servants, having left that morning. Except for the matter of the draperies not being drawn, however, Colley was glad he had gone. Although Cark had not been there long, for he had only recently replaced gentle old Edwards, who had retired from their family's service, Colley did not like him. He thought Cark had shifty eyes, and was certain he considered waiting on a puny boy not quite eleven a degrading nuisance.

Not one of the several grim-faced gentlemen in their somber black suits who had come to the house seemed to find it necessary to explain to Colley why Cark or any of the other servants had been let go. Of course, Colley did not care much anyway as long as there was someone he liked left to look after him. And he liked Lucy Tripp. Lucy was his former nursery maid, now proudly promoted to lady's maid. But unlike Colley, she had a great many opinions about what was happening in the household. Her lips had been set grimly as she threw back the covers of Colley's bed that evening.

"Wonder is Mrs. Whitley and I are still here, though someone has to be left to look after you. But doesn't seem right making such changes so sudden when your dear mama and papa have only just been . . ." She stopped suddenly, seeing the look on Colley's face. Her eyes softened.

"I'm sorry, Master Colley. I mustn't be talking like that. You've already been through such a bad time. You don't need me making it worse. But though I know your mama and papa can't ever be brought back, things will be better when your uncle and aunt come. Pity is it's taking such a long time to find them, traveling here and there about the world as they are. But by now they must have the sad news and will be on their way back. They're certain to arrive one day soon."

"Well, I don't want them to arrive one day soon, Lucy!" Colley burst out. "I don't want them to arrive *ever!*"

Lucy shook her head in shock and dismay. "Oh, Master Colley, you musn't say such a thing. Why your Uncle Jasper is your dear papa's very own brother. What would your papa have said if he could hear you?"

"Well . . . well . . . I don't care!" Colley flung back. "How can

I be expected to like Uncle Jasper when he doesn't like me? Nor Aunt Serena either. Oh, they pretend to like me. They pat me on the head and call me a good boy, and bring me a present at Christmas. But it's all put on. I know it is. I don't think either one can bear to be around me. And now I'm to live with them. Oh, Lucy, I don't want to! I don't want to!" Colley's voice caught in his throat, and he threw his hands over his face to hold back the tears stinging his eyes.

"Master Colley, you musn't go thinking you're not liked," Lucy said gently. "Everything will turn out all right. I know it will. I'm still here, aren't I? And I'll do everything I can to see I'm kept on. I'll be looking after you just as I always promised your dear mama I would, every time she went out, worried as she always was you would come to harm while she was away."

For several moments the room was filled with a deep, sad silence. For both knew that in the end it was Colley's mama who had come to harm, and his papa as well, when on a simple evening out, their carriage had met with a dreadful, fatal accident. They were both no more, and Colley was left an orphan.

"I . . . I don't care," Colley blurted at last, "I don't want to live with Uncle Jasper and Aunt Serena. Why . . . why couldn't I just come to your house and live with you, Lucy? I'm certain they don't want me and would be glad to have me gone."

"Oh dear, Master Colley!" Lucy could not hold back a rueful smile. "*You* living in the small cottage I share with my ma and pa when I'm home, after all you're used to here? I have a grand picture of that, I do! You wouldn't be allowed to come visit, much less live there, no matter what you might think."

"Then . . . then perhaps I could go live with Jonas," Colley said brightly, Jonas Winkle being his tutor and someone whom he liked very much. "I could have lessons every day, and . . ."

"Master Colley, you musn't be silly," Lucy interrupted. "It's here that you're going to stay, and you will be just fine."

"No, I won't! You don't have to keep saying that. I'm not going to stay here, not with those people who don't want me!" Colley flung back his head defiantly. "And I'll tell you what I'm going to do, Lucy. I'm going to run away like . . . like Jeremy did. Yes, I am! And there's no one can stop me!"

Jeremy was Colley's cousin, his Uncle Jasper's son and Aunt Serena's stepson. Many years older than Colley, he had disappeared when Colley was an infant. Whether Jeremy had actually run away or met with foul play, Colley was never certain. All he knew was that his parents had only spoken of Jeremy on rare occasions, and then in such a way that Colley knew he was not intended to hear them. Jeremy, as far as Colley knew, was also never mentioned in the presence of Uncle Jasper and Aunt Serena.

Lucy's face was stricken upon hearing Colley's threat. "Master Colley!" she cried. "You'll do nothing of the kind! How can you be thinking such a thing? Where would you run to, pray tell? And think how frail you are and how very nasty and cold it is outside. Think what it would do to your poor chest. And oh, Master Colley!" Lucy threw a hand to her mouth, stifling a gasp of horror. "What if you got lost wandering about in the dark, and then fell into the river, so swollen now from the rains. I really don't want to hear another word said about running away!"

"Well . . . well, all right then. But . . . but I still *am* thinking about it," retorted Colley, who naturally was doing no such thing. He was not such a dunce as to disagree with a word Lucy said. He just needed someone to know how unhappy and desperate he felt.

"Well, you may just stop thinking of it at once!" said Lucy, throwing him a fierce frown as she removed from his table the supper tray she had brought up earlier. "And see how you've just picked at your supper. You will remember to take your spoonful of tonic before you go to bed, won't you?" she asked anxiously.

Colley was not at all certain he would do this. The tonic had a terrible, fishy taste, and did little to improve his appetite as it was supposed to do. Nor was it doing anything else to improve his life that he could see. Besides, why improve his appetite anyway? If he was not to be allowed to go live with Lucy or Jonas Winkle, he might just try starving himself to death. But, of course, there was no use in telling Lucy all this, so he simply replied to her question with a dutiful nod.

"There's a good lad!" said Lucy. "And don't forget you're to ring if you need anything, anything at all." Then, with an attempt at a cheerful smile, she left the room.

As soon as the door had closed behind her, Colley dropped down into his armchair, turned up the oil lamp, and picked up his book. But somehow, what with the howling wind and the tall windows staring at him, he could not keep his mind on the story he was reading.

Why, he wondered, had he not thought to ask Lucy to help him draw the draperies while she was there? He felt too ashamed now to ring the bell and summon her from the distant servants' quarters. After all, had he not threatened boldly and bravely to run away? How would it look now for him to cry for help with something so small and ridiculous as pulling a curtain? He would just have to manage it himself. But Colley, for all his nearly eleven years, had arms much too thin and frail to pull the cords of the heavy draperies. After several futile attempts, he gave up in despair.

Finally, as he lay in his bed, in an effort to drown out the sound of the wind, and hide from the windows he knew were there, he threw his covers up over his head. And that is how, miserable, lonely, and frightened, he fell asleep at last.

Colley stirred restlessly in his sleep, feeling as if he were suffocating. Then, halfway awake, he somehow remembered having pulled his covers up over his head, although what was over his face now did not feel at all like his fine, soft cotton sheets, or his light-as-air down comforter. This felt more like rough wool—scratchy, heavy, and smelling thickly of must and mildew. Could it be part of a bad dream he was having?

He tried to reach up to pull the cover off his face, but found he could not lift his hands. Next he tried to move his legs, but found them held down as well. He began to feel truly frightened and started to struggle.

"Lucy! Lucy!" he made an effort to call out. But something came down heavily like a clamp over his mouth, so not much more came from his throat than a strangled squeak.

"That'll be enough of that!" a man's voice, low, harsh, and menacing, snarled in his ear. "If you know what's good for you, you'll keep your mouth shut tight. Do that and don't try something smart, and you won't get hurt. You get that?"

Colley most assuredly did get that, and made an attempt to nod his head. For the effort he received a rough shake along with a reminder.

"Well, see you don't forget it," the man growled.

Colley's covers were then ripped off him, and the coarse wool blanket pulled down to cover his whole body. A rope was jerked around his waist and tightly knotted, making certain that he was firmly imprisoned.

"Dip, you get his feet, and I'll get the shoulders," the man ordered. "I'll douse the lantern, then let's get out of here."

"What about his stuff?" the man addressed as Dip asked. "Ain't we gonna take any of his clothes?"

"Don't be a jackass," the first man growled. "What makes you think he'll be needing them where he's going?" He gave a sour laugh.

"Well, maybe he won't, but look at them shoes. Look at the stuff on the chair. And that overcoat over there would fetch a penny or two, I'll tell you. Aw," Dip whined, "why can't we take the stuff?"

"Oh, all right then," came the grudging reply. "Put the shoes on his feet so they won't drop and make a racket, and the rest on top of him. But be quick about it."

Colley felt his shoes being roughly shoved onto his feet, without courtesy of any socks. Something understood to be his clothes was thrown down on top of him. Then his ankles and shoulders were grabbed, and he was swung from his bed. Moments later he felt himself being carried down the stairs of the house.

Even if the blanket over his face were not all but shutting off any air, his heart was thumping so hard from fright that he could hardly breathe anyway. And as for crying out, had he dared, who would have heard his muffled voice? Gampet, the head groom and one of the only remaining servants, would be asleep in his quarters over the stables. Lucy and Mrs. Whitley, the cook, were the only ones left in the house, and the two of them so far distant in their rooms they could barely have heard someone screaming at the top of his lungs, if at all. There was nothing Colley could do but allow himself to be carried as if he had no more voice or life than a sack of potatoes.

He knew when they left the house, for he felt the wind biting through the blankets wrapped around him. Then he heard the crunching sound of the men's boots grinding heavily down into the gravel outside the house. When the crunching sound stopped, Colley knew they had left the circular driveway. Silent, except for an occasional oath as they stumbled on a rock or bare root in the darkness, the men now stumped down the long driveway leading to the massive iron gates of the fence surrounding the Trevelyan estate.

Whether they actually reached the gates, Colley had no way of knowing, but he did at last hear the sound of horses snorting and the restless clinking and chinking of their harnesses. Hinges squealed as a door was opened, and Colley felt himself hoisted up and shoved onto a hard floor. Moments later one pair of heavy boots, and then a second, brought their owners up to where he lay.

Then the two individuals dropped down with a grunt, their boots carelessly kicking into Colley in the process. A door slammed shut, the sharp crack of a whip sliced the air, and wheels began to rumble as the carriage, for that indeed is what now imprisoned Colley, began to roll forward slowly, then rapidly picked up speed.

"Should we unwrap him?" the voice belonging to Dip asked.

"What do you have in your head where brains ought to be?" came the reply. "The boy's not blind, is he? Do you want him knowing you if he ever sees you again?" The voice paused briefly. "I didn't think so, if you know what's good for you. Anyway, I'm going to try to get some sleep. It's a long ride back to the city. Let's hope we get there before daybreak."

With further deep grunts, Colley's traveling companions arranged themselves for sleep, their boots digging into him with no less concern than if he had, in fact, been a sack of potatoes. In no time their snores thundered over his head, a hideous accompaniment to the drumming of horses' hoofs and rolling wheels as the carriage rumbled through the night.

A Foolish, Foolish Threat

Colley had now learned that he was being taken to the city. But to what special place in that enormous city was he being taken? And by whom? And most puzzling, and perhaps most frightening of all—Why? Why? Why? The questions whirled crazily in Colley's head as he lay on the floor, his body aching and bruised as he was pitched back and forth by the swaying carriage lumbering over rutted, rocky, country roads.

This would be a long and horrifying journey, if indeed they were headed for the city. Before arriving there from the Trevelyan estate, Colley's home, a traveler must pass at least two small townships. Colley remembered only once ever having been taken to the city, and that was when he was a small boy. Frail, just as Lucy had said he was, his parents had never seen fit to take him again. But he still remembered what a long and tiring journey it had been, and how huge and frightening the city had seemed. Tall buildings crowded together so you could hardly see the sky, sidewalks teeming with people, tradesmen quarreling in loud, angry voices on the street, children screaming, horses snorting, and dogs barking. Looking through the window of the carriage as it bowled through the streets, Colley had clung to his papa's arm in fright.

Still, how comforted and coddled he had been on that journey, wrapped in warm blankets with a soft pillow placed under his head when he became tired, and fed arrowroot biscuits and sips of hot, sweet India tea when he was hungry or thirsty. He might now be going to the same city, but oh, how different this journey was from the last one!

Thump! Thump! Colley groaned as the wheels of the carriage hit a large rock, but the sound was lost in the thunderous snores of the two men and the pounding of horses' hooves. Who was it taking him to the city *this* time? Who were these villainous men who had stolen him from his home? All he knew of them were their voices, and those heard through the thickness of the rough wool blanket over his head. One voice, the one belonging to the man who appeared to be the leader of the two, seemed unnaturally deep and gruff, as if he were trying to disguise it. But why bother to disguise it if it belonged to no one Colley knew anyway? Or—or was it possible that he did? If so, who of the people Colley knew was the owner of that voice?

Names, first one, then another, leaped into his head, each dismissed as too improbable to consider. Actually, there were very few names that Colley could even put faces to. Tutored at home by Jonas Winkle, he had no schoolmates or any other friends, although he sometimes played with Hugo and Duncan, who came with their parents to visit. But both of them were sturdy, rough-and-tumble boys who had no interest in Colley's books and quiet board games. They were apt to tease and torment him because he was always the loser at catch or tag or racing across the lawn. But then, it was no boy he must think of, but a grown man.

Other than his parents, his tutor Jonas Winkle, and Dr. Gravely, who came to tap Colley's chest regularly, and then shake his head in a despairing manner, Colley knew very few grown-ups. He was almost always summoned from his room to be presented to friends of his parents when they came to visit, or attend a garden party or ball; but after bowing stiffly and shyly upon being introduced, he was always glad to escape back to his room. As a result, he knew none of his parents' friends and acquaintances, and so had none to add to the small list of names parading miserably through his head.

In truth, most of the people he knew well were the household servants, but it hardly seemed possible that any one of them would be capable of committing such a crime as this. Some of them had been with the family since before Colley was even born. And while it was true that almost all of them had recently been dismissed, Colley could not believe any one of them would return to harm him. But he had no sooner had that thought, than he stiffened, drawing in his breath with a sharp gasp. For a name that had lain there in his head all along, silent and sinister as a snake coiled up on a forest floor, suddenly struck out at him. Cark!

Cark—so new to the household he could have little loyalty to the family. Cark—who had made little pretense of having much use for Colley. Cark—who on his last visit to Colley's room before he was dismissed, had darted a cool, appraising look at Colley through heavy-lidded eyes. It had made Colley's skin creep for some reason, but he had forgotten about it until now. And finally, it was Cark, the head butler, who would know the most about what servants were gone and when it was safe for him to return. As for keys to the house, he had no doubt either kept them or had copies made. How easy it was for him to return to carry out his dastardly plan. Cark!

Cark! Cark! Cark! The horses' hooves drummed out the deadly name.

But then came the question—why? What did Cark, if it were in truth he, intend to do with Colley? Murder him? Well, did he not all but say that Colley would need no clothes where he was going? Were not his clothes stolen right along with him only because of the money they would fetch?

Murder!

Yet what did Cark have to gain by murdering Colley? Simply not liking him was hardly a reason for risking the hangman's noose. No, there must be another reason, and what other could there be than—money. Ransom! That must be it—Colley was to be held for ransom.

But with his parents gone, who was there left to pay it? It would have to be Uncle Jasper, who was to be Colley's guardian, and Aunt Serena. They, however, were still away on their travels, and it might be days, perhaps weeks, before they would arrive home. Still, Cark would know this, and know that he must be prepared to wait. And—Colley's heart sank at the thought—so must he.

Thump! Thump! Thump! Shivering uncontrollably, for after all he was covered only by his thin nightclothes and one blanket, Colley now hurt all over. It seemed that it hardly mattered that he might have a wait at the end of his journey, for he might never even get where he was going alive.

But if he did, perhaps he might not have such a long wait after all. Would the police not start their search for him at once, just as soon as Lucy discovered him missing in the morning? Kidnapping would naturally be the first thing suspected. Colley knew from remarks made by Lucy that she liked Cark little more than he did, so might she not suspect him at once just as Colley did?

Thump! Thump! Thump! Once more Colley let out a small cry, but not this time from pain. For he had just remembered something—his very own words uttered a bare few hours earlier.

"I'll tell you what I'm going to do, Lucy. I'm going to run away like . . . like Jeremy did. Yes, I am! And there's no one can stop me!"

Oh, what a ninny he had been! How he wanted to take back those foolish, foolish words! For they were exactly what Lucy would report to the police, that and how she feared Colley might fall into the swollen river.

If only his clothes had been left behind, a kidnapping might still be suspected. For Colley would hardly be expected to have run away on such a murderously cold night in no more than his nightshirt, not even wearing shoes or an overcoat. But there were the shoes on his feet, and all the rest of his clothes sitting, no doubt, on the seat by the two villains. So it seemed that the police would be hunting for Colley in the wrong places until they received some notice from the kidnappers demanding ransom. And undoubtedly that would not come until they were certain Colley's uncle and aunt had returned. It might be a very long time before he was rescued, a very long time indeed. And what was to happen to him during that time? Where was he to be kept? Who would look after him? And what new terrors would be in store for him?

Run away! Run away! Stupid! Stupid! Stupid! The words drummed on and on through Colley's aching head. How could he have been so stupid? How could he have actually said such a half-witted thing? Could he not have just thought about it, if only to make himself feel better, and not have uttered the words?

Stupid! Stupid! Dim-witted! Pinheaded! Colley began calling himself every possible thing he could think of. Stupid! Stupid! Brainless! Half-witted! Idiot! Imbecile! Mooncalf! Saphead! And when he had completed the list of all the names he knew, most of them learned from Hugo and Duncan, he began all over again. But no matter how many things he called himself, or how many times he repeated them, nothing could unsay the words, "I'm going to run away." Nothing!

Chapter III

The Broggin Home
for Boys

The carriage drew to a stop at last, and Colley was once again treated to the pleasure of having two pairs of heavy boots jabbing into him as the men shoved themselves out the door. Then, with no more ceremony than when he was dumped inside, he was dragged back out again, although only halfway, with his shoulders still resting on the carriage floor and his legs dangling outside. The squeak of pain he let out was silenced by a sharp rap on the head.

"Shut up, you!" The command came in the low, ugly voice now known by Colley to belong to the butler Cark.

"We leavin' his stuff out here?" Dip asked.

"We are if we ever expect to see it again," came the quick reply. "Meese is keeping the carriage here until we get back."

"How about the boy's shoes?" asked Dip. "Do we leave them here too?"

"Why not? None of his stuff came with the deal, shoes included," Cark replied. "But let's get on with it. Here, I'll give you a hand."

Colley felt his shoes being yanked off his feet and some skin from his ankles along with them. This time, however, he knew bet-

ter than to make a sound. *Thump! Thump!* His shoes landed, one
following the other, back into the carriage. Then he was dragged
the rest of the way out, and once again felt himself being trans-
ported by the two villains. To where? And to what? At least the
grim carriage ride appeared to be over. It did not seem to Colley
that anything could be as bad as that. At the very least, he might
soon be having the smothering blanket removed, and he could see
again. It did not much matter to him what he looked upon as
long as he was no longer imprisoned in that suffocating darkness.
Lugged a short distance on level ground and then up several steps,
Colley heard a bell jangle, muffled and distant as if deep inside a
building.

"You sure they're expectin' us this time of day?" Dip asked.

"When else would we be coming with this kind of delivery,
in the bright sunshine? You dolthead!" Cark snorted. "Of course
they're expecting us. Don't think they don't know how everything's done. It's their business. Now, don't you go—"

He stopped at the sound of a door handle turning, and a door
opening. "We've got the goods," he growled under his breath.

"They're waiting for you," a nervous voice replied. "Follow
me."

The parade made up of the two men and their "goods," otherwise known as Colley, started up again. "You just keep your
mouth shut like you've been doing," Cark hissed into Colley's
ear. "We'll be setting you up on your feet. You stand there nice
and proper, and don't try anything smart."

"In here," the same nervous voice directed them.

A moment later and Colley was set upright, his feet hitting
chilling linoleum. Cramped from being bound and lying for so
long in one position, aching all over and stiff with cold, it was too
much for him. His knees buckled, and he started to crumple.
Steely fingers immediately snapped around his arms on either side,
jacking him up.

"Come from having too sound a sleep, I'll warrant," said Cark in a tone of voice suggesting he was addressing someone deeply concerned with Colley's welfare.

"But I see he has no shoes," a woman's voice said sharply.

"Well . . . well . . . well . . . ," Dip began to stammer.

Cark cut him off with lightning speed. "No, no shoes. Not dressed either. He's just in his nightclothes. We didn't dare take the time."

"Didn't you bring any of his things along with him, an overcoat perhaps?" a man's voice asked.

"Oh, no!" replied Cark, sounding shocked at the question. "We couldn't take the time for that either. We just left everything behind."

Left everything behind? Yes, behind on the carriage seat, a carriage still awaiting these two villainous men right outside the front door. And they were standing there, bold as you please, lying to two warmhearted people who cared that Colley was barefoot and needed shoes and warm clothes. A sudden flash of burning rage swept over him, overcoming his dread of his two kidnappers. He must report their lie at once to his two new benefactors! And would not such caring people protect him against punishment by these criminals?

Swiftly he drew in his breath and began, "But they—" It was as far as he got.

The steely grips instantly tightened around his arms, and from behind came a jab in his ribs so hard it silenced him as surely as if a cork had been rammed down his throat. Further, the blanket had deadened his feeble attempt to such a degree that no one else in the room must have heard so much as a squeak.

"Well," the woman said, "aren't you going to remove the cover so we can see him?"

"Begging your pardon, Madam," Cark said, "but we'd as soon be gone before that happens."

"As you wish," the man said. "So as all transactions are now concluded, there appears to be no further reason for you to remain. Soup, will you see the men out?"

As the footsteps left the room, Colley waited hopefully to be released from his blanket prison. And waited. And waited. But no one came over to remove the blanket, and all around him was only silence. Had the kindly man and woman stepped out for a moment? Perhaps they had gone out with the others, which explained why Colley had not heard their footsteps leaving. But they would return soon, he was certain, for anyone with such tender feelings would know how dreadful it was for him to be tied up as he was. Such sympathetic hearts would not want him to wait a moment longer than necessary. But more moments did pass, and at last footsteps entered the room. A single set of footsteps. Whose were they?

"Get that thing off him, Soup, so we can have a look at what we got," the man said, his voice coming from the same direction it had come from before.

"And do be quick about it," added the voice of the woman. "We might yet get a minute or two of sleep before morning."

Had the two of them been there all along doing nothing to relieve Colley of his misery? Why? Were both of them perhaps crippled and unable to move? And why were the fingers of the person now known to be Soup trembling as he struggled to undo the tight knot in the rope tied around Colley.

"Come, come, don't be all day about it, Soup," the woman said, and Soup's fingers trembled even more, thus becoming clumsier than ever.

But at last the knot came undone, the rope slid to the floor, and the blanket was dragged off Colley. Now, what he had wanted was happening at last. The grim carriage ride over, he was being released from the blanket prison and could see again.

It took a few moments for his eyes to adjust to his surroundings, but only a few, because the room he found himself in was deep in shadows. What light there was came from two small oil lamps fluttering weakly on the wall. Tiny tongues of light licked feebly at a barren pine desk, two unforgiving straight-backed pine chairs, and an older boy, as much a skeleton as the chair he stood beside, distinguished by his ownership of a long, thin, sallow face, a hunched back, and one leg vastly shorter than the other.

But what was of greater importance to Colley were the man and woman, both in night-robes of some dreary dark color, planted in front of the desk, arms folded, silently staring at him. These must be the two benevolent people who cared that Colley was without shoes or overcoat. But if he had not been certain that these were the two very same people, he might have had some difficulty in believing it.

Was it possible that any soft words could have found their way through the woman's lips, now compressed into a cruel, hard line, or any tender looks have come from those glaring, cold eyes? And what of a nose and chin that appeared sharp enough to crack granite? As for the general facial setting in which these objects were located, why, it was so shriveled that any warm blood visiting there must surely have long since departed. Even the pink ribbon decorating the night bonnet that crowned this vision, was so limp and dejected one might think that, having allowed itself to be placed there, it now deeply regretted the error.

The man who stood beside her was remarkably short and squat, barely reaching her shoulder. His face, in keeping with the rest of him, was likewise short and squat, with nothing about it close to resembling any human face Colley had ever seen before.

Was that mushroom-shaped item compressed and spread across his face actually a nose? If so, then what was stretched almost from ear to ear like a rubber band must have been the mouth, though its lips were so thin as to be non-existent. As for a chin, he owned nothing that could be properly described as that either, for a wide expanse of flabby white flesh descended straight from his mouth, making it appear that there was no neck joining head to body. Over all these items was a pair of black beady eyes, half shaded with thick, suspicious eyelids. If the face of this man could have been compared to anything, it would have had to be that of a toad, although in any beauty contest, the toad would surely have come off the winner.

Still, whatever their appearances, these were the two who had taken pity on Colley's condition. Should he not try to show them how grateful he was? Somehow, he managed to produce a trembling smile.

The smile was not returned.

Instead, although his head never turned so much as a fraction of an inch and his eyes remained fixed on Colley, the man now spoke, but it was to the woman beside him. "And what is your opinion, Mrs. Crawler?"

The woman, Mrs. Crawler, likewise kept her staring eyes fastened on Colley as she replied. "No doubt, I am sorry to say, the same as yours, Mr. Crawler. Not good for much. Of course, considering the terms of the transaction . . ."

"Exactly!" said Mr. Crawler. Then his eyes narrowed even further. "Do you know where you are, boy?"

The tone of the words left no doubt that a smile was no longer required or of any value. It left Colley's face in an instant as he shook his head.

"You've been brought to the Broggin Home for Boys where you will be schooled, fed, and clothed, and for all of which blessings you will be expected to work." Mr. Crawler paused to let this information settle in before continuing.

"We are Obadiah and Quintilla Crawler, proprietors of this institution. We desire you to now take particular notice of the fact that we are not going to ask *your* name. Further, we are never going to ask your name. Would you care to know why?"

By now Colley could not have uttered a word, for his tongue was frozen to the roof of his mouth. He was barely able to nod.

"We—are—never—going—to—ask—your—name," said Mr. Crawler, drawing the words out and appearing to relish saying each one. "We are not going to ask your name, boy," he repeated, "because we don't want to know what it is. We are *never* going to want to know what it is. Nor do we want to know anything about you, not who you are, or where you come from. None of that matters to us, for as far as we are concerned, you have no past. *None!* All we care about is what you are right now, and forever after, and that's a Broggin boy. Soup, will you study the list and refresh our memories on who's been crossed out lately?"

"Yes, Mr. Crawler. At once, Mr. Crawler!" One foot dragging, Soup limped hurriedly to the desk, there pulling out a drawer and lifting out a shabby dark green notebook. Clumsy from his eagerness to carry out the order, he was finally able to find the right place in the notebook and run a shaking finger down a page. Then the finger stopped. "Here's Jed. *He's* crossed out."

"Ah yes, Jed," said Mr. Crawler. "Well, that will do. No need to go further. Unless *you* have an objection, Mrs. Crawler."

"None at all," she replied. "Jed's as good as any."

"Your name, then," said Mr. Crawler, directing his attention back to Colley, "is henceforward to be Jed. And as every boy here bears the last name of Broggin, you will likewise. Now repeat after me—Jed Broggin."

"J-J-Jed B-B-Broggin," stammered Colley.

"Again!" snapped Mr. Crawler. "You'd better do better than that."

"J-Jed B-Broggin," repeated Colley.

Mrs. Crawler's eyes flared. "It won't do, Mr. Crawler."

Mr. Crawler's mouth tightened around his teeth. "Again!" he spat out.

Colley swallowed hard. "Jed Broggin," he said slowly and carefully.

"That's right," said Mr. Crawler. "Jed Broggin. Anyone asks

you, that's what you tell them. Jed Broggin. No remembering any
name you used to have. The day you do and we hear about it will
be the day you'll wish you'd never been born. And remember
this well, the one you trust the most might be just the one you
can trust the least not to come running right to us. Others have
learned that to their sorrow. Now, Mrs. Crawler, have you anything you wish to add?"

"Just mind him well, Jed Broggin. Mind him well!" This
menacing warning from Mrs. Crawler hardly needed the accompanying flaring of her eyes to chill Colley to the marrow of his
bones.

"Soup, you can take him to his bed. You know which one,"
Mr. Crawler said.

"Oh yes! Oh yes!" Soup replied eagerly. "Number nine-
teen . . . I know which one."

"And you'll see he has clothes by his bed before the rising
bell?" said Mr. Crawler, more by way of a command than any
question.

"Oh yes, I'll see to that, Mr. Crawler. Yes, I'll see to that," said
Soup, so anxious to please that one word stepped right on the
heels of the next. Beckoning to Colley, he half ran, half walked to
the door, his one foot dragging along on the floor.

By now it was certainly clear to Colley that he need no longer
be concerned with producing any smile. Shivering with cold, for
he was after all still clad only in his nightshirt, and had nothing
between his feet and the cold linoleum, and so paralyzed from
fright he could barely move one leg after the other, he trailed after
Soup. With every step he took, he could feel on his back the piercing eyes of the couple who were the proprietors of the Broggin
Home for Boys, the kindly caring, sympathetic, tender, warmhearted Obadiah and Quintilla Crawler.

Chapter IV

Jed Broggin

Directly outside the door, Soup stood with a small oil lamp dangling from one shaking hand. Although the lantern produced only the barest of fluttering lights, it was enough to tell Colley that they were in a hallway as cold and bleak as the room they had just left, featuring dingy brown linoleum and walls of a sickly faded green. A network of cracks and stains from grime and grease were a cheerless reminder that a large number of years had passed since the walls had been visited by a coat of paint, or received any other attention. One stark, unpainted wooden bench directly across from the door appeared to be the only furnishing in the room.

"Where you sit and wait if yer called," Soup said under his breath, his eyes darting nervously from side to side. It appeared that it was necessary to conjure up for Colley the picture of a trembling Broggin boy sitting there stiffly in mortal fear as he awaited an audience with Mr. and Mrs. Crawler.

But then Colley saw what might have been considered a second article of furnishing. It was a portrait hanging on the wall across from the bench.

"That's them watchin' you whilst yer waitin'," Soup pronounced solemnly.

It was indeed a portrait of "them," and if it were possible to make the subjects appear any worse than they were in person, the artist seemed to have managed it. But what he also managed to do was provide them with the kind of eyes that, while fixed, followed the viewer no matter where he stood—or sat. So it seemed that whether on the bench or off it in that hallway, a Broggin boy was never out of sight of the proprietors of the Broggin Home for Boys. Colley felt the eyes boring into his back with every step as Soup led him toward the narrow, steep stairs rising precipitously up the right-hand wall.

Just before they reached the stairs, however, Soup turned left unexpectedly, leading him through a set of double doors. And Colley then felt another shock, for they were once again being stared at by the deadly painted eyes of Obadiah and Quintilla Crawler! It was yet another portrait of the two, larger and uglier than the first, looming on the wall. The light from two small gas lamps set one on either side flicked over the likenesses, making them even more ghastly, as if that were thought to be necessary.

Instead of staring at one solitary bench, however, the eyes now kept guard over a cavernous room featuring one very long table, seemingly made up of several tables drawn together, with wooden benches drawn up to it. The end of the table opposite the portrait was laden with precariously tilting piles of mismatched pottery bowls, rows of tin cups in varied sizes and conditions, and a tangled heap of spoons, mostly bent.

The whole unappetizing dining scene was enhanced by the thick smell of overboiled cabbage mingled with that of disinfectant soap. Remaining stale smells were provided by a row of jackets in assorted sizes—all well worn, some to the point of being little better than rags—hanging from nails in a row down one wall.

"Where you get fed," announced Soup, a curious note of pride suddenly appearing in his voice, as if a boy should somehow be impressed by the room and by actually being allowed to eat in

it. Then he waved a hand in the direction of a tall cabinet looming in the shadows of one corner of the room, and added with an
important air, "and do everything else as well."

All Colley could think was that the "everything else" must be
yet another horror. But Soup chose to say nothing further about
it, and Colley was left to guess what it was as they left the room
and entered yet another. This one, at least, was not graced by pictures of the two owners.

"Kitchen," reported Soup, as if the iron stove and great black
pots and pans dangling from the walls and ceiling did not make
that clear enough. But once again Soup waved a hand, this time in
the direction of an open door by the stove, leading off into darkness. "Scullery," he said. "You ever worked in one?"

Worked in one? The truth was that Colley did not even know
what it was. He had never been allowed to roam into the kitchen
at Trevelyan House, and had been there on only two or three occasions with Lucy. Nothing had ever been mentioned about such a
place as a scullery.

"I . . . I don't think so," he stammered.

Soup shrugged. "You'd know if you had. But it ain't a surprise
if you ain't, wearin' a fancy nightshirt like the one you got on.
Well, you'll find out 'bout it soon enough."

Already shivering from the cold, Colley gave a violent shudder. A grim bench in the hall. A foreboding cabinet in a dismal
dining hall. And now something with the ominous name of
"scullery" that he was to know about soon enough.

Horror upon horror upon horror, in a night already filled with
horror! Was there more to come? When Soup led him from the
kitchen into an evil-smelling back entry, and then down, down,
down a perilously steep set of cold, damp stone steps, Colley felt
as if he were being led down to a dungeon or—a tomb. By now,
that could hardly be surprising!

But when at last he had stumbled off the last steep step onto a rough stone floor, equally cold and damp, he saw by the flickering light of Soup's lantern that they were in another hallway. *Thud, shhhh. Thud, shhhh.* Guided by the feeble light of the swinging lantern and the sound of a dragging foot, Colley followed Soup past a closed door to a doorway appearing to be no more than a black hole in the wall. Soup jerked his head at Colley, and entered it.

They had come into a room barely large enough to hold six narrow iron cots in two rows of three each against the walls. Hanging on the wall by all but one cot were what must have been clothes, or what passed for clothes at any rate, for in all but one lay a boy, now dead asleep. To the empty cot at the far corner of the room, Soup led Colley.

"This is yers," he said, waving the lantern over the cot. "In the mornin', which ain't too far off now, there's a bell goes off. Then you jump faster'n you ever dreamed were possible, pull up yer bedcovers, and jump into yer clothes. Then you go with the rest to the facilities, which is up the stairs at the other end of the hall and through the door. That's the play yard likewise. No dawdlin' there neither. After that you get on up to the dinin' room where you were just at." Soup paused, raised his lantern, and with appraising eyes studied Colley from shoulders down to his bare feet. "All right, now I got yer size, you can get into bed. I'll be right back with yer stuff. Clothes hangin' on these here nails by yer bed. Shoes and socks under it."

Thud, shhhh. Thud, shhhh. Soup and his lantern departed the room, leaving Colley in darkness thick as pitch to clamber under the rough wool blanket that was the only covering the cot provided, and lay his head down on the small, hard lump that passed for a pillow. But he did not have long to lie there, rigid and shivering, before Soup, as announced, was back with the "stuff," otherwise known as clothes. Silently he went about hanging these up on the two nails provided for the purpose, finally shoving under the cot what had to be the shoes and socks. Wearing a satisfied look on his face, he shone his lantern around the room, and then left without another word, taking every shred of light with him. Once again, Colley was left alone in the darkness. Or as alone as possible when taking into account the fact that there were five other boys in the room with him.

Five boys! Five boys who, if they were anything like Hugo and Duncan, would be five teasing, taunting, tormenting boys. And they would not be boys who would return to their homes when an afternoon of play had ended. No, they would be right in the room with him, living with him. Five boys! He could hear them snuffling in their sleep around him. Was this the final horror? What more could there be?

Clamping his jaws together to keep his teeth from chattering, Colley drew his feet up under his nightshirt, and pulled his blanket tightly up around his chin, just as he had done when he had climbed into his own bed earlier that same night. Then, however, it had been with cotton sheets and a down comforter. Under his head had been a cloud-soft pillow for him to burrow into. Now around his chin was a coarse wool blanket that bit into his skin. The small, hard lump of a pillow already made his head hurt and his ear grow numb. Only a few hours had passed since he had been in his own cozy bed, but oh, what a difference those few hours had made! How could so many terrible things have happened to him in such a short time?

He had thought that when his mama and papa had been in an accident, and were suddenly no more, nothing worse could ever happen to him. But grim as that had been, at least he had been safe in his home with someone to look after him and care for him.

How easy it had been to make bold, brave threats about running away when he sat in a room with a plush Persian rug under his feet, a room furnished with softly gleaming mahogany bookcases and tables, a handsome four-poster bed, and a comfortable leather reading chair set before a splendid fireplace with burning embers crackling and dancing under a carved oak mantelpiece. And all he had had to worry about was the glare of tall glass windows over which he could not draw the velvet draperies! No wonder Lucy had shown such horror at the idea of his running *anywhere*.

What dismay and disbelief would Lucy feel if she were to know of his being dragged from the house in only his thin nightshirt, and of having to walk on stone cold floors in his bare feet. He remembered the words she had used, "Think how frail you are! Think what it would do to your poor chest!" He had always hated hearing such things said, even though they were probably true. How often he had wished never to hear them again. Well, now he might get that wish, for who was there to care enough to say them? Would Mrs. Quintilla Crawler note sadly how he "only picked at his food"? Would Mr. Obadiah Crawler kindly remind him that he must remember to take his spoonful of tonic?

But there was something Colley knew he could tell himself over and over—all this horror was not going to last. For once the villainous Cark had received the ransom he demanded, Colley would be returned to his home. And there was no question now that he had guessed right about being held for ransom. Were not the sinister words "terms of the transaction" spoken by Mrs. Crawler proof of that?

Why Cark had chosen such a grim place for him to be kept while waiting to be ransomed, Colley could not guess. But no prison could have kept him more secure. He had been warned that nobody there cared who he was or where he came from. He was now just another Broggin boy, and if he ever told anyone otherwise, it would be the day he wished he had never been born. And who, remembering the glaring, venomous eyes of Mrs. Crawler, or the hideous toadlike stare of Mr. Crawler, could doubt that no iron bars or heavy padlock could do a better job of keeping a young boy safely imprisoned? Certainly not Colley Trevelyan.

No! No! No! With a sudden jerk, Colley pulled the blanket even more tightly around his chin. His eyes darted from side to side in terror. For though he could see nothing in the deep, suffocating darkness, there was also nothing to say those terrible eyes were not there piercing his very brain and knowing everything in it. He must no longer even *think* the name he had grown up with. Jed Broggin—that is who he was now. And if he wanted to save his skin, to still be alive when he was finally rescued, he must remember that. But for how long? Days? Weeks? Oh, how was he to bear it?

Jed Broggin. Jed Broggin. Jed Broggin. Remember it! Remember it! Jed Broggin. Would he remember it when he awoke later? What if he did not? Well, he would not fall asleep. He would stay awake saying it over and over again. Over and over. Jed Broggin. Jed Broggin. Jed Broggin. Colley never knew how many times the name had marched through his head before his weary eyelids drifted shut, and the marching stopped at last.

Chapter V

A Hateful Nightshirt

*B*rrrannng! Brrrannng! Brrrannng!

The sharp, ear-piercing jangle of the bell crashed through the darkness of the cellar room like shattered glass. With a violent start Colley awoke, his heart hammering. For a moment he could not remember where he was, nor imagine what the terrible noise was that had awakened him. But then the dread memory of all that had happened swept over him. With a shudder he remembered where he was—in a room with five other boys—and what Soup had whispered to him—that in the morning a bell would go off that would rattle his teeth. Well, the bell must have been what awakened him, but how could it be morning? The room was as dark as it had been when he had crawled into his cot, with not a flicker of light anywhere. And furthermore, around him all was silent. Then—

Brrrannng! Brrrannng! Brrrannng!

The bell jangled again. And now the silence was suddenly broken by the sound of rusted cot springs squeaking and bare feet thump, thump, thumping on the ground. Colley knew that he must climb from his cot as well, and quickly. Shivering, he dropped his feet down onto the icy stone floor. How he was to find the clothes hanging on the nails and put them on in the dark, he had no idea, but he remembered that he must pull up his bedcover. That, fortunately, was something he could manage. As he reached down for it, two oil lanterns suddenly flared up. They were at the opposite end of the small room, but cast enough dim light that Colley could see all five other boys. And they could see him, or might have if they had not been so intent on scrambling out of the shapeless gray flannel nightshirts they all wore. But one boy did see him, one with curly black hair in the cot next to his.

Just before the nightshirt went up over his head, he caught sight of Colley, then dropped the nightshirt back down again. For a moment he stared at Colley with an odd look of disbelief on his face. Then with a jerk of his hand he beckoned to the other boys, now swiftly buttoning on baggy trousers, their pale, thin chests still bare.

"Hey, come see wot we got usselves here—a flippin' girl!"

The four other boys, dragging over their heads ill-fitting shirts of assorted drab, faded colors, lost no time in making their way over to join the first boy, the lot of them staring at Colley with wide, equally disbelieving eyes.

"Yer right, Marty," agreed one of the boys, one with brick red hair, a carpet of freckles the only color on his pasty face. "It really are a flippin' girl. Where do you suppose it come from? And wot's it doin' here?"

"Ain't got no idea, Noah," replied Marty. "Anybody else got one? Rufus?"

The stubby-haired, sallow-skinned boy addressed as Rufus shook his head.

"Toby?" asked Marty.

The boy called Toby sniffed, flicking a knuckle across his stub nose. "I ain't heard nothin' 'bout it."

"Zack?" Marty asked the remaining boy.

Zack widened a pair of washed-out blue eyes, then threw out his hands and shrugged. "Whyn't you just ask it?"

"Faith, Zack, 'cause it don't appear to have no flippin' tongue," replied Marty. "So far, it ain't said a word."

The subject of this discussion did, of course, have a tongue, but it was frozen so tightly to the roof of his mouth that for all useful purposes he might have had none. He was further struck dumb by the fact that he was trembling violently under his nightshirt, and terrified lest the boys should discover it. So all he did was stare ahead like a rabbit caught in the glare of a carriage lamp. But he knew he must say something. He must!

Praying that no one could hear the quaver in his voice, he took a sharp breath and managed to blurt out, "I . . . I do have a tongue! And . . . I'm not a girl!"

"Sure, an' if ye ain't no girl, why are ye wearin' all them fancy ruffles on yer nightshirt?" Marty asked, exchanging telling glances with the other boys.

Colley's nightshirt did in truth have ruffles around the neck and at the cuffs, but he had never thought a thing about it. Until now he had never seen any nightshirts but his own, and for all he knew, every one was like his, and every one was provided with ruffles.

"I . . . I . . . I," he stammered, and then came to a stop. Having seen the ugly gray flannel nightshirts of the others, confessing that he had believed all nightshirts to be like his might get him in even more difficulties. And in this he was not far wrong.

"Wot kind of people got nightshirts like that?" redheaded Noah asked. "Where'd you come from anyway? Oof!" His eyes popped as Marty gave him a swift, sharp dig in the ribs with an elbow. "Hey, wot'd you do that for? I ain't done nothin'."

"Sure an' ye know we ain't supposed to ask no questions like that," Marty said, scowling at him. "Where's yer brains gone?"

"Sorry, Marty," Noah said, biting his lip.

"All right, then," said Marty. "Ain't nothin' we get to know but wot he's called. Wot name is it they give ye?" he said to Colley.

Colley's recital to himself that night now came to his rescue. "Jed Broggin," he said instantly, proud he remembered it.

But he had no sooner said the name than he saw the other boys look uncomfortably at Marty, whose eyes suddenly darkened strangely. Then he lifted one bare foot and shoved Colley's cot angrily.

"Them murderin' creeters had to give out *that* name, didn't they?" he said between clenched teeth.

"We ain't never had it happen since we all been down here, so we don't know but wot it's how they allus does it, Marty," the boy named Rufus said gently.

Zack, his pale blue eyes deeply mournful, nodded. "That's right. Easier to keep us all straight, maybe."

"Faith an' they could o' waited," Marty said. His voice broke, but he quickly swallowed hard and tightened his jaw. "An' look wot's got the name, a Mister Sissy Ruffles. Look at him. Don't know where he come from, but looks like he ain't even been teached to wipe his own nose. Don't know why we're standin' 'round here. He ain't worth any o' us gettin' the hole on his 'count. Let's be off!"

Without so much as a second look at Colley, the boys swiftly scattered and began throwing on socks and shoes, and in Marty's case, his other clothes as well. Colley was left standing alone, his eyes now stinging dangerously. So far, for all the misery he had endured, except for the first night after he learned of his mama and papa's dread accident, he had shed no tears. Now he was perilously close to doing so. Yet he could certainly guess the result of the boys seeing himself dissolved in tears. He must not let it happen.

But there was something else he must not let happen, and that was to be late. Soup had issued a warning about it. And though not directed at Colley, but at the other boys, so had Marty. The hole! It appeared that if they were late, they would get something called "the hole." Mr. Crawler had said something about a day

Colley might wish he had never been born. Would the hole be part of that day? It was something Colley had no wish to find out.

Quickly he snatched the ugly nondescript garments from the nails on the wall, then tore off his nightshirt and, with shaking hands, scrambled into the baggy trousers and a rough gray shirt that fit him not much better than any flour sack would have. The shoes he dragged from under his bed, shoes measured for his feet only by Soup's appraising eye in a darkened room, were hard, murderously uncomfortable, and far too large. He could not have kept them on had it not been for the socks of heavy, rough wool that filled a good portion of the space not occupied by his feet. With clumsy, cold fingers he somehow managed to tie the laces of the shoes.

Looking up, Colley saw Marty, the last boy to finish dressing, about to leave the cellar room. Then, just as Marty stared through the doorway, he hesitated, reached out, and carefully turned off the two lanterns hanging from hooks on the wall. This left Colley to make his way through the dark room to the doorway with only the dim lights from the three tiny gas lamps in the hallway to guide him.

Oh yes, Colley saw how it was to be in that cellar room. It was all very clear indeed!

Chapter VI

A Ghastly Meal

S oup might very well have saved whatever breath he had in his thin, hunched chest when he warned Colley against dawdling in "the facilities." For while a washbasin was provided in the cellar hallway in the form of a long iron tank with faucets jutting out over it, the remaining facilities were outside. These took the form of dank wooden stalls, blackened and stained, set against one wall of an enclosed square of packed dirt measuring no more than a dozen and a half feet on each side. A narrow, steep iron stairway, crawling like a black centipede down the wall of the Broggin Home for Boys, was evidence that these facilities were used by both the upstairs as well as the cellar inhabitants. Had Soup actually used the words "play yard"? How could those words describe this rank, dismal little square of property, so guarded by the tall brick buildings surrounding it that no ray of sun could ever have reached it, or any breeze carried in a breath of fresh air?

Colley, being the last boy to enter one of the stalls, ended up being the last one to leave, so found himself alone in the deserted yard. His heart pounded with fright as he raced back into the cellar, up the stairs, through the kitchen, and finally into the dining hall.

While dawn had not progressed enough to provide any light

through the three tall narrow windows at one end of the room, the two small gas lamps noted earlier were now joined by three ugly flaring gas ceiling lamps. By their light Colley saw some two dozen boys, all but a handful of whom stood behind the benches that lined the tables, faces pale and pasty, hands dangling motionless at their sides. Other than being in an upright position, these deadly silent boys gave very little evidence of even being alive.

On the table in front of each one lay a tin cup, a spoon, and something in a bowl that might or might not have been porridge, thick and sickly gray in color. But there was no question as to its origin. For at the end of the table nearest the kitchen stood a bald man of vast proportions, his florid round face featuring a swollen, heavily veined nose, and the rest carpeted with a dense black beard. His bulging front was wrapped in a filthy apron, presumed at one time to be white under the grease and other assorted food stains. With arms thick as posts and hands large and red as slabs of ham, he was ladling the sticky contents of a large iron pot into a bowl held by Soup. This was then handed to a boy waiting in line for it. There were still four boys in line when Colley arrived. Four boys only, but enough to keep Colley from arriving to find no line at all. Breathless, he joined the line, keeping his eyes firmly locked on the neck of the boy ahead of him.

But as he stood there, he began to notice something curious. Something eerie. It was not the flaring gas lamps, nor all the boys, nor even the unpleasant individual dishing out food. What he now noticed was that other than the clink of the ladle against a bowl, or the sound of a boy carrying his bowl to the table, the room was silent. Deathly silent. As he waited for his bowl to be filled, Colley stole a quick sideways look down the room. And found himself looking directly into the eyes of Mr. and Mrs. Crawler!

The eyes of Mr. and Mrs. Crawler in the painting. The eyes of Mr. and Mrs. Crawler in person! For the two of them stood directly under the painting. Four pairs of cold, cruel, pitiless eyes sharp as screws being twisted into the brains of every boy there. And to think that Colley had actually believed himself safe because some boys were still in line for their food when he arrived! Oh yes, those eyes would not have missed seeing him arriving late. And it was certain that this event had been duly registered.

Thump! Thump! Thump! Colley and his too-large shoes now provided the only sounds heard in the silent room as he made his way with bowl, spoon, and cup to the place Soup pointed out to him as his. When he arrived there, his hands were shaking to such a degree that his bowl and cup rattled on the table when he set them down. This was undoubtedly noted not only by the Crawlers, but by the boys nearest him, who turned out to be the five from the cellar room.

When at last no further sounds, except breathing, were to be heard in the room, Mrs. Crawler clasped her hands and raised her eyes upward. "The blessing, please, Mr. Crawler," she said.

Mr. Crawler, as opposed to Mrs. Crawler, kept his hooded eyes securely bolted to the boys, not trusting to any higher authority to do the job for him, it appeared. "For this food which you are about to eat, you had better be grateful."

When this dubious message had been delivered, Mr. Crawler then tapped a tin cup three times with a spoon, a sign for the boys to scramble onto the benches and seat themselves at the table. But there was still no talking or whispering or laughing or any other sign of liveliness. After three more taps on the tin cup by Mr. Crawler, the boys picked up their spoons and began silently to shovel heaping spoonfuls of porridge into their mouths. Mr. and Mrs. Crawler, apparently denying themselves the pleasure of shar- ing this sumptuous meal with the boys, sat with hands folded, glaring at them as if to ensure that they were indeed grateful for every spoonful.

Colley had no interest whatsoever in the porridge. But he knew that he was expected to eat it. He took up the spoon and hesitantly put a small amount in his mouth. And it was all he could do not to spit the gluey, ghastly, tasteless lump right back out again. He could not eat this horrible concoction. He could *not*. He would starve to death first!

Well, was that not what he thought he might try the very night before? How easy it had been to produce such a thought when he had just been served a meal of tender chicken breast, tiny buttered peas, potatoes in a delicate cream sauce, and for dessert a sugary, spicy, baked apple. And this morning would he not have been certain of a tenderly poached egg, a delicious hot muffin, and a dish of sparkling sliced oranges? In the future, if there was to be one, he would never, *never* have such a thought again!

Then Colley saw something that lightened his spirits considerably. Being passed down the table on both sides were tin pitchers. They, of course, would be filled with milk, perhaps even cream. With the help of that on his porridge, he could get down a spoonful or two. But as a pitcher drew closer, he saw that what the boys were pouring into their tin cups was nothing but water. So at the end of the meal, Colley was left with the full bowl and the fervent, though dim, hope that this had not been registered by the sharp eyes of Mr. and Mrs. Crawler.

When three more taps on the tin cup signaled the end of the dismal meal, the boys all left the table, taking their cups, spoons, and empty bowls, and leaving them at the end of the table. This done, they all hurried to the jackets hanging on the wall, threw them on, but remained standing in place to form a line heading for the doors to the hallway. Colley set his bowl down with the others, relieved that Soup, still at the same post, did not remark on the fact that it remained full of gray porridge.

"That's yer jacket, ten from the left," Soup whispered to him. "You put it on, an' pull out wot's in the pocket. Then you stay in line like the rest and do wot they do."

Colley was relieved that he could find the jacket, put it

on, and join the line without drawing further attention to himself. It did not matter at all that the jacket was two sizes too big for him, that it had frayed cuffs and holes at the elbows, and never had had the benefit of a cleaning, though doubtless having been worn by another Broggin boy. Was it not safer that way, to look like the rest of them? What if the whole lot knew of the nightshirt with ruffles? It was not something Colley wanted to think about too long.

The jacket on, he reached into the pocket and pulled out something resembling what the other boys held in their hands, a rag best described as being well used and filthy. The line of boys moved toward the door, and as each one arrived there, he held out the rag to the bald, bearded man who had earlier ladled out the porridge. Now he stood with a tin tub in his arms, from it doling out lumps of bread, one into each rag held out to him. The boys then folded the rags around the bread lumps and stuffed them into their pockets. Colley did the same when his turn came, wondering if the bread was part of their breakfast, and when they would eat it. It, at least, looked like something he could swallow.

When he entered the hallway, he found that the line had broken up. The boys were forming silent clusters around three men standing there waiting for them. Colley remembered that Mr. Crawler had said there would be "schooling." Could it be that these men had come to escort the boys to a school? Colley hesitated, not knowing if he were expected to join a group, and if so, which one. Suddenly he felt a set of fingers snap around his arm.

"All right then, come with me!" Colley's head jerked around, and he found himself looking directly into the eyes of Mr. Crawler!

Walking so quickly that Colley in his oversize clumping shoes could not keep up with him, Mr. Crawler half dragged him to a group of boys gathered around the man standing nearest to the front door. As this might have something to do with schooling, Colley half expected to see someone resembling his tutor, the pale, bespectacled, gentle Jonas Winkle. What, in fact, he now saw before him was a burly man with shoulders that could only be compared to those of a bulldog, and a coarse, mottled red face, round and flat as a plate. At least two days' worth of stubble sprouted in uneven patches around his thick, wet lips and bulbous, pitted nose. As Mr. Crawler dragged up the terrified Colley, the man's red-rimmed eyes fixed him with a hard, calculating stare.

"This the one?" the man asked.

"The one, Gorp," replied Mr. Crawler. "Delivered as promised."

The man called Gorp reviewed Colley again with narrowed eyes. "What name did you give it?"

"The name's Jed," replied Mr. Crawler.

"I might have figgered that. Makes life easier, don't it?" Gorp's thick lips widened in an evil grin.

"Indeed it does, Gorp. Indeed it does," said Mr. Crawler. "And here's its paper, all done up nice by Grimpot and company."

Gorp snatched the folded piece of paper handed him by Mr. Crawler and jammed it in his pocket. "All right then, boys, let's git off!"

He flung open the front door, standing aside as the boys trooped out. "That means you too, Jed," he snarled at Colley, who stood there too petrified to move. "Git goin'!"

The fear of what might be the end result of his not obeying was enough to send Colley quickly clumping through the door with the other boys, none of whom were from the cellar room. Not that it would have made any difference if one of them had been, for he would have paid no more attention to Colley than the rest. But Colley could see as they trudged along that though the boys were as weary and beaten down and silent as they had been at the table, each one appeared to be a friend to the one beside him. Colley alone had nobody.

It was still dark out, but oh, what a terrible picture the gaslights revealed to Colley! The city he remembered had been a fearful enough place, but this seemed far worse. And now he was not in the devoted care of his mama and papa with a carriage window between him and the sights, sounds, and smells, so grim, harsh, deadly—and frightening!

No, he was out in the open, trudging up one street and down another with a rough individual named Gorp and a pack of silent boys, not one of whom gave a sign that he cared if Colley were alive or dead, or even there at all. To one side of them loomed buildings of brick blackened with dirt and soot, and held together with crumbling mortar. On the opposite side of the cracked, filthy sidewalks ran rivulets of something too unspeakably filthy to bear the name of water. Darkened windows looked down with blank unseeing eyes on this pitiful parade of young boys. Nor did any of the pale, pasty-faced men and women, all intent on their own misery as they crept from their doorways, pay any more attention to the boys than if they were the ash cans, the scraps of filthy paper, or the rags and broken bottles that littered the sidewalks.

When the parade of boys stopped at last, it was before the battered doors of a low-roofed tin building encrusted with black soot. Several large windows were spread across the front, but were filmed with dust and dirt so thick their usefulness to admit light was doubtful. And when Gorp opened the doors to let the boys in, a blast of murderously broiling hot air hit them in the face.

Colley found that they had entered a vast room so thick with fumes and dust he had to gasp to draw a breath. And there was not a desk, not a blackboard, nor any book in sight, so any thoughts of this being a school were gone in a moment. All there was, was terrible heat and the glaring light of fires roaring in rows upon rows of open furnaces. The floor was littered with broken glass, a silent testament to the fact that this was a glass factory. And what would Colley and all the other boys be there for if not to work before these deadly furnaces?

Horror upon horror upon horror. Was it never to end? Who had done this to Colley? And *why*?

Chapter VII

A Mysterious Disappearance

A gluey, gray, slimy mass of cold porridge sat accusingly on the table before Colley. It was now the evening meal, but the same bowl of porridge that had sat before him that morning sat before him now. When he had lined up with the other boys to receive his supper bowl, he had been handed the porridge. It was clear to him, even without Soup's whispered warning, that he would be having this same porridge served him forever if he did not eat it, every last horrible bite. The sharp, watchful eyes of Mr. and Mrs. Crawler would see to that!

What the others had been served was a kind of stew, mostly potatoes it appeared, with some odd bits of something of uncertain origin swimming around in a sickly pale gravy. It hardly looked very tempting, but whatever it was, it could not have been worse than the cold porridge.

Since the evening before when, just as Lucy had said, Colley had "picked" at his supper, he had had nothing to eat. Nothing, that is, unless two bites of the stale bread that had gone wrapped in a dirty rag in his pocket to serve as his noonday meal—as it turned out—could be considered "something." But it was a wonder he had even managed those two bites as, in the few minutes allowed them to eat, he had crouched on the glass factory floor with the fires from the furnaces roaring at him, his face burning from the blasts of heat, and his throat choking with dust and fumes.

Now he picked up his spoon and took one small bite of the cold porridge. He could barely choke it down, but he finally took another bite as well. Then he lay down his spoon. There was no way that he could manage a third bite. Yet it was not just because the porridge was so sickening to swallow. It was that his chest hurt, that his eyes stung, and that there was hardly a bone in his body that did not feel as if it were going to break in two. And he was so tired he could barely hold his head up. If only the meal would come to an end so he could go down and fall into his cot. And oh, to be able to fall asleep and have sleep erase all memory of that terrible day.

Then at last he saw that bowls were becoming empty and heard the clink of spoons as the boys scraped up the last sickly drops of stew. But before Mr. Crawler had administered the three taps of the spoon on a tin cup to signal that the meal had ended, he beckoned to Soup, who went hurrying up to him. After a brief conference, Soup came rushing as fast as his dragging foot would allow to where Colley sat.

"Yer to do scullery duty now with Silas," he said. "You remember I pointed out where it was." Then he dropped his voice. "Said you'd find out 'bout it soon enough."

Moments later, Colley, along with the boy called Silas, who had been one of the other Broggin boys at the glass factory, was staggering back and forth from the dining hall to the room known as the scullery, loaded down with tipsy stacks of bowls, and trays holding tin cups and spoons, and finally, with himself on one side and Silas on the other, the black kettle that now held only the stiffening remains of the Broggin boys' evening meal.

Scullery! The very word, especially as it had been presented by

Soup, had a cruel sound to it. And for Colley that night, it was a cruel place indeed! It had no roaring furnaces blasting out murderously hot air to burn and blister the lungs and fill them with deadly dust and fumes. But it was a rank, dimly lit, dingy, cold, damp, small room featuring two large iron sinks sunk into a wooden counter, blackened with age and grease, and hardly an inch of it not scarred with knife wounds. As he stumbled in with the final load, near to fainting, Colley collapsed against the wood counter. This was the end. He could not move a muscle to do one thing further. It was all he could manage just to hold himself up.

Silas, rolling up his shirt sleeves, looked at Colley and shrugged. "Looky here, first day at the glass works ain't easy. I seen you gettin' water splashed in the mug four times to keep you goin'. Me? I only got it twicet my first day." This revelation was delivered with a hint of a swagger. "But ain't none o' it easy, no time, no how. So I'm all wore out too. An' I ain't got no plans to do all this work with just me and no help from you. You been restin' long enough, so roll up yer sleeves, and let's get movin'. I ain't got no interest in spendin' the night here."

Colley stared hopelessly at the stack of dirty bowls and the iron kettle. "H-h-how should we begin?" he stammered, wondering if he could muster the will to begin at all. One thing was certain, there was to be no more sympathy from Silas than he had received from anyone else since he had looked on Lucy's worried face the night before.

Silas ran his fingers wearily through his lank brown hair and sighed. "How we does is like this. I worsh half, you rinse. Then we switches. Then we share on the kettle. After that, both o' us wipes the lot with them rags over there, an' take it all back where it come from." He paused to turn on one of the faucets over the sink and ran a practiced finger through the water dribbling out. Then he shook his head resignedly. "Ain't hot enough. Never is. We got to use soap, more's the flamin' bad luck."

•   •   •

Nearly an hour passed, for it seemed they were expected to sweep and clean the kitchen as well as do the dishes and kettle. Soup arrived to inspect their work, informing them that one potato peel was left sitting on the floor, and if not picked up, Boiler would let them have "what for." Boiler, it appeared, was the thick-necked, bearded individual who doled out food at the table. Considering the filthiness of Boiler's apron and general appearance, Colley wondered at his caring about one potato peel on the floor, but he knew better than to mention it. Nor at this point, being more dead than alive, did it matter much to him. But at last Soup declared the job done.

"An' if you ain't goin' to dawdle," he said to Colley, "you can make it to yer room 'fore the lights get put out. I ain't comin' with you 'cause I already done my check down there an' you already know yer way. Just don't make no mistake an' go into the first door. It's Boiler's room, an' he don't like no one comin' in on him."

Barely able to drag one foot after the other, Colley crept from the kitchen as quickly as his aching body would allow him. As it was, he had barely reached the bottom of the steep cellar steps when the gas lamps in the hallway, dim at best, flickered and went out altogether, plunging the hall, and Colley along with it, into total darkness. And even though he had been certain he could find his way to his room, that certainty evaporated with the light. Stumbling, he reached out for the wall, feeling his way along it until he came to the door to his room. To his surprise, he found it closed. But why should he be surprised? Was it not one more sign of how the boys felt about him, closing the door on him?

And then, suddenly, a great blast of sound came from behind the door. It was a roiling, rumbling, gurgling sound of vast proportions, something akin to the sound of water being sucked down an enormous, powerful drain. Terrified, Colley jumped backward. Then the sound came again, and now he recognized what it was.

Confused by the darkness, he had forgotten Soup's warning and almost entered the first door, where he would have run right into Boiler, asleep and—*snoring!* Quaking in his too-big shoes, Colley continued down the dark hallway.

To his relief, he found the next door open, and the soft breathing sounds told him that this was not only his room, but that the boys were all in bed and asleep. He somehow managed to make his way to his cot, and was relieved to make another discovery. Just by feeling it, he could tell that his miserable ruffled nightshirt had been replaced by the standard ugly item of rough gray flannel. Then, though his hands felt as if all the skin had been peeled off by the harsh yellow soap provided for use on the dishes, he managed to drag off his clothes, climb into the nightshirt, and finally drop like a stone into his cot, able to go to sleep at last.

To sleep? Oh no, no, never believe such a luxury was yet to be allowed him! For the moment he closed his eyes, his brain began to spin. Round and round and round, always asking the same question—Why? Why had he been put here, and how long could he survive in such a place? He was still certain he was being held for ransom, but could he live through the few days until his rescue.

Unless he had been thoroughly hoodwinked by the Crawlers, how could one as sharp as Cark not know what might happen to a boy left in the loving care of the Broggin Home for Boys? Could Cark have been so stupid as to believe that one such as Colley could come out of it alive? And how much ransom would Colley be worth if he were to end up being delivered in a pine box? None of it made any sense. None!

Round and round and round. Would his brain never stop spinning? How he envied the other boys in the room sleeping so peacefully. Though they each lived the grim life of a Broggin boy too, perhaps they were used to it. After all, he had seen how Marty and the others all lapped up their porridge and dreadful-looking stew, leaving not much but the bowls when they were finished. But more than that, they had each other, friends, companions, partners. Perhaps you could survive being a Broggin boy if you had that. But Colley did not. He had nobody!

Round and round and round. Round and round and round. And then all at once he heard a curious sound.

Sssst! Sssst!

Colley's eyes flew open, but he could see nothing in the darkness.

Sssst! Sssst! There it was again!

Then from somewhere in the room came the sound of a whispered voice. "Is he asleep yet? Marty, can you tell? He asleep yet?"

Colley heard the sound of bare feet thumping softly to the floor from the cot next to him and quickly snapped his eyes shut. Then he heard what must be Marty padding stealthily over to his cot, so he started to breathe deeply and slowly, as if he were in a sound sleep. He could feel Marty lean over the cot and breathe on his cheek. Then he heard Marty padding away.

"Ain't able to see his eyes, but sure an' he's asleep all right," he whispered. "Ain't nobody breathes like that wot ain't asleep."

A low conversation then took place, too far from Colley's cot for him to hear what was being said. Then Marty's voice rose a little. "Come on then, ye lot. Let's go!"

Colley opened his eyes a crack, enough to see that a lantern had now been lit. It was turned down so low as to be almost not lit at all, but still gave enough light for Colley to tell what was happening.

While one boy, Zack, held the lantern, Marty reached under the middle cot, and grunting softly from the effort, appeared to be moving something that made a scraping sound on the floor. He then reached up, took the lantern from Zack and, after turning up the flame, crawled with it under the cot. He did not reappear. Instead, one by one, silent as animals in a forest, each boy disappeared under the cot. There came the scraping sound again of something being dragged on the floor, and the dim glow from the lantern coming from under the cot was instantly gone. Now all that was left in the room were the empty cots, darkness, and silence.

Where had they all disappeared? Surely five boys could not be huddled together under one small cot. And even if they could manage it, what would be the point of it? To hold a conference? About what? Colley? To laugh about his ruffled nightshirt? To talk about how he, unlike them, was one who had never even been taught to "wipe his own nose"? To tell each other how they wished he had never been put in that room?

And then Colley thought suddenly of that odd sound—the sound of something scraping across the floor. Could it be the cover to some small underground room—or a *tunnel?* A tunnel! A tunnel possibly leading away from the Broggin Home for Boys! Could that really be it? And were the boys escaping? Were Marty and Noah and Rufus and Toby and Zack going to be free?

They must have been planning this all along, and not been too delighted to have Colley show up in the room. Still, they had clearly decided to go ahead with the plan anyway. But why could they not have included Colley? Well, did he really need to ask himself that question? Why would they have been so dim-witted as to include on such a dangerous venture someone who wore ruffled nightshirts and, in their opinion, did not even know how to take care of his own nose? Not to mention being someone they hardly knew, and in any case, certainly did not like? So Colley had been left behind—alone. Alone—and faced with the prospect of having to explain what had happened to the rest!

Would he be rewarded for his goodness in not going with them? Hardly! Was it not more likely that he would be asked why he had not come to report the escape as soon as he knew of it? Better just to say he had been asleep and had no idea of what had been going on around him. In other words—lie! But lie before

Mr. and Mrs. Crawler with their accusing, cruel eyes piercing into his very brain? Why, he would be turned into a stammering, guilty-looking bowl of quivering jelly in a matter of seconds. What, oh what was he to do?

Well, why not escape himself? Escape! That would mean crossing the room and climbing down a steep ladder, all in total darkness without benefit of any lantern. Then it would mean making his way down an equally dark tunnel, perhaps with dank walls and slippery puddles of foul water underfoot. And were not tunnels the hiding place of vicious rats? It was a terrifying prospect.

And if he made it safely, what then? The boys would not have tried anything so daring if they did not have some place safe to go. And where could Colley end up? Whom could he trust with his story? "The one you trust the most might be just the one you can trust the least not to come running right to us." That was the chilling warning delivered by Mr. Crawler. What chance did Colley have outside the walls of the Broggin Home for Boys? He would quickly be brought back to face something far worse than what he had already faced.

Yet what could possibly be worse? What more could they do to him than had already been done? Beat him until he was no more? Yet was that not how he was going to end up as it was? He must risk it. Yes, he must, and he *would!* And at last, with his heart lodged securely in his throat, Colley put a tentative toe out from under his cover, ready to climb from his cot. But then he quickly drew it back in again.

For suddenly, he had heard the same scraping sound come from under the middle cot. A moment later a lantern light reappeared, followed by Zack. Then, one by one, the boys slipped quietly out from under the cot. The scraping sound came again, and the lantern light went out. The boys' feet were heard padding back to their cots.

"'Night, Marty!" came a whisper from across the room.

"'Night, Noah! 'Night, ye all!"

"'Night!"

"'Night!"

"'Night!"

There was the sound of creaking springs as five boys climbed back into their cots. Then deep silence once again fell in the cellar room.

Where had the boys gone? And why had they come back? Colley could not begin to guess. All he knew was that he had been left alone before they went. Now they were back, and he was still alone. The last thought he had before sleep that finally put an end to all thinking was that everything was just as it had been. Nothing had changed at all.

Chapter VIII

The Telltale Penny

The next morning the boys paid no attention to Colley at all. No one even appeared to notice that he was now wearing the same gray flannel nightshirt as the rest of them. Or at least, if anyone did, it was certain that no one said anything about it. Colley was left to exchange his nightshirt for his shirt and trousers in silence. Nobody looked at him, and he tried not to look at them as well. It seemed, after all, as if there was nothing he could do to change how they felt.

There was still, however, one thing he could try to do. That was not to be the last one to arrive in the dining hall that morning. And though hurting all over and by now weak from hunger as well, he somehow managed to dress quickly enough to find boys still in the yard when he arrived there, and boys arriving behind him in the food line. If only he could have done something about the meal itself. Once again he was presented with the same bowl of porridge, by now almost as hard as the bowl itself. He could barely dig his spoon into it, and three more bites was all he could manage. He told himself that he would do all he could to swallow the stale lump of bread at the noon meal, even if it had maggots running through it, and never mind the blistering heat from the furnaces, or the dust or the fumes.

But there was one thing Colley had not counted on: that the grim day at the glass factory could become even grimmer. What he had done the day before was remove half-finished bottles from molds with heavy, unwieldy tongs. Gorp had informed him it was the easiest job in the factory, and yet, just as Silas had said, Colley had indeed had water dashed in his face four times to keep him from fainting dead away over this "easiest job."

How many dashes of water would he have had in his face if instead of "take-out boy" he had been given the job of "carrying-in" boy and had to carry three or four red-hot bottles at a time on a huge shovel to be gradually cooled in yet another oven. "Carrier pigeons," Colley had heard these boys called. Oh, what a lovely, friendly sounding name for such a terrible job!

When Colley arrived for work that day at the glass factory, Gorp announced to him that he would be doing something different. "It's a promotion, you might say, Jed," he said with a leer that announced just what he thought of the promotion he was about to bestow. "You're about to take a hand at bein' a little carrier pigeon! Ain't that nice?"

Ding, ding, ding, ding, ding! Ding, ding, ding, ding, ding! The sound of Mr. Crawler's spoon beating on the tin cup suddenly rang out in the dining hall. This was not the usual three beats signaling the end of the meal, nor were the boys finished emptying their bowls of evening stew. Nonetheless, they all set their spoons down, every head swiveling with fixed, wary eyes to face Mr. Crawler. Every head, that is, except the one belonging to Colley, who sat seemingly paralyzed in his seat. He had not set his spoon down in his bowl either, because he had never picked it up in the first place, being half dead—no, more like three-quarters dead—when he had arrived there. All the while he had just sat motionless, with his eyes fixed vacantly on the remaining lump of porridge before him.

"Pockets!" The word exploded from Mr. Crawler's thin, wide

mouth as if he had been keeping it locked up and savoring it for the whole meal. His flabby white chin veritably quivered with the relief and delight of releasing it.

Immediately, the boys scrambled from their seats and stood silently at attention before each place. Colley's numbed brain at last relayed the message that he had better do as the others did, and he struggled up from his place at the table.

"All right, *now!*" snapped Mr. Crawler. "Let's get those pockets out!"

The boys immediately thrust their hands into their trousers' pockets and pulled them out. Anything that might have been hidden in the pockets was then laid on the table beside each bowl. Still in a daze, Colley pulled out his own trousers' pockets. They were empty, of course, but others around the table were not. Pitiful evidence of young boys' interests appeared on the table—a bent nail, pebbles, a bit of dirty string, bits of filthy paper.

There was only one thing that was dug from a pocket that had any value at all. It was a penny. It was not bright, not new, and was tarnished and dented, but nonetheless—a penny. It had come from Marty's pocket, and it now lay by his bowl. Well, not quite by his bowl. Since he sat next to Colley, it now lay halfway between his bowl and Colley's bowl, or close enough to halfway that who could tell the difference? A penny! A miserable little penny! But at that moment it was as important as a ten-dollar gold piece or a glistening diamond.

At the head of the long table, Mr. and Mrs. Crawler slowly and deliberately rose to their feet. "Are you ready, Mrs. Crawler?" asked Mr. Crawler.

"Oh yes, quite ready!" replied Mrs. Crawler.

The two of them then proceeded down the sides of the table, Mrs. Crawler, with hands folded before her, taking one side, and Mr. Crawler, with hands behind his back, taking the opposite, Colley's side. But both sets of narrowed eyes were doing the same thing, darting sharply from place to place, from object to object that had found its way to the table from some hapless boy's pocket. Slowly, slowly, the Crawlers made their way down the room. *Tap. Tap. Tap.* And then Mr. Crawler's footsteps came to a stop. They stopped directly behind where Colley and Marty stood. Across from them, Mrs. Crawler froze in her steps, an icy statue with eyes fastened on Mr. Crawler and his two victims. A terrible, expectant silence fell in the room. It seemed the very walls had stopped breathing.

"And what have we here?" Mr. Crawler stretched his hand out between the two boys and pressed a fat thumb on the table in front of the penny. *Thump! Thump! Thump!* went the thumb, three times before being withdrawn with a snap, as if someone might be actually going to steal it from him.

"It does look to me like *money*. Would you not say it looks like money, Mrs. Crawler?"

"It bears a powerful resemblance to it, Mr. Crawler," replied Mrs. Crawler, staring tightlipped at the offending item.

"And where, Mrs. Crawler, has it ever been written that a Broggin boy was to be the possessor of money?" asked Mr. Crawler.

"Why, nowhere, Mr. Crawler—nowhere," replied Mrs. Crawler.

"And yet, Mrs. Crawler, it seems that a Broggin boy has seen fit to write such a rule himself. The question being, which one?" Mr. Crawler paused to slam his fist down on the table so viciously that the penny flew up and returned trembling to the table. "Now I expect a confession at once. Who is it who claims to be the possessor of this money?"

Was it a minute passing? An hour? A year? A century? It did indeed seem so, but it was actually no more than the time measured by a few quivering heartbeats before a voice spoke out.

"It's . . . it's . . . it's me, Mr. Crawler!" It was the dazed, quavering voice of Colley.

A few more heartbeats were permitted to pass for the remaining inmates of the room to digest and ponder what might be the consequences of this terrible confession. "Did you hear that, Mrs. Crawler?" said Mr. Crawler at last. "It is Jed, our newest boy, who has admitted to this crime." He put his mouth so close to Colley's face that Colley received the full effect of a breath that might well have come from an inhabitant of a swamp. "And where, may I ask, did you obtain this money, Jed?"

"I . . . I . . . I . . ." Colley floundered.

"Well? Come, come—where?" said Mr. Crawler menacingly.

"I . . . I found it on . . . on the street," blurted Colley.

"And, of course, put it right into your pocket instead of see-ing that it came to Mrs. Crawler and me!" said Mr. Crawler. "What do you think of that, Mrs. Crawler? A Broggin boy fallen into evil, thieving ways and not here two full days. The question is, what are we to do about it, eh? Would you suggest a touch of the hole might be in order, Mrs. Crawler?"

Through lips tightened over set teeth, Mrs. Crawler sucked in her breath with pleasure. Her hard eyes glittered with anticipation. "Oh yes, Mr. Crawler, most certainly a touch of the hole!"

"Well, then, if you will remain to do the honors, Mrs. Crawler?" said Mr. Crawler as charmingly as if they were all at a tea party.

"Oh certainly, Mr. Crawler," said Mrs. Crawler equally charm-ingly, with a look on her face, however, that let the boys know they could expect as much "charm" from her as they might from a rattlesnake.

Then—snap! Colley felt Mr. Crawler's hand grabbing the back of his shirt collar and heard Mr. Crawler's voice bark in his ear, "Now, move!"

Half walking in his clumping shoes, half being dragged by his collar, and certain that his shaking legs would give out on him at any moment, Colley was led by Mr. Crawler from the dining hall, through the kitchen, past the scullery, down the cellar steps, up the cellar hallway to the very end, where at last they came to a stop.

Only then did Mr. Crawler let go his hold on Colley's shirt collar, but not without giving it a violent shake.

"See you don't go anywhere!" he growled.

Go anywhere? Colley was now about as able to "go anywhere" as a tree stump while he watched Mr. Crawler remove the padlock from an iron grate in the floor. The hinges on the grate squealed as he lifted the grate to reveal a gaping black hole. Breathing heavily from that effort, he lifted a lantern from the wall, lit it, and held it over the hole.

"All right," he snarled, "You get on down there, and be quick about it!"

A moment later the trembling Colley was clutching the rungs of a steep iron ladder, while trying to keep his clumsy shoes from slipping off as he climbed down, down into a black pit. Mr. Crawler held the lantern over the opening just long enough for Colley to reach the bottom and discover that he was now in a cold, clammy space, reeking of mold, and only large enough for a boy to sit or lie down. Either of these had to be accomplished on the floor, for there was barely enough room for the boy, much less furnishings of any kind.

Mr. Crawler had no sooner determined that Colley had arrived at his destination than he doused the lantern and barked down the hole. "Well, Jed, perhaps you'll learn now how we do things at the Broggin Home for Boys!"

The hinges groaned, the iron grate clanged down, the padlock snapped shut, the key turned in the lock, and Mr. Crawler's boots pounded down the cellar hallway. The sound of them finally disappeared to leave behind a deadly silence. To all intents and purposes Colley was *entombed* in the lowest reaches of the loving, caring Broggin Home for Boys!

Chapter IX

A Gummy Bun

Ssst!

The sound was followed by silence.

Sssst! Sssst!

More silence.

Sssst! Sssst!

Colley, lying on the floor of the hole with his knees drawn up and arms wrapped around himself in an attempt to keep warm, heard the sounds and stiffened. Was it the hissing from some underground snake crawling around over his head? Or did the sound come from humans? Could they mean some new torment was in store for him? Holding his breath, he listened for the hissing to come again. Instead he heard whispered voices.

"Think he's dead?"

"Couldn't be."

"Well, he ain't sayin' nothin'."

"Might just be asleep."

"I think more likely dead."

"I say he ain't. Sssst! Sssst! Jed! Jed! Ye alive down there? It's meself, Marty."

Marty!

Though cold, frightened, hurting, and imprisoned at the bottom of a black pit, Colley was still curiously able to feel a flash of anger at the sound of the name. Marty! The boy who had so far given no sign that he felt anything but hatred for Colley. Marty, who seemed to be the one influencing all the others to feel as he did. Marty, who had pushed the telltale penny so far over on the table that Colley had no choice but to confess to its ownership. Why not just let him and the other whisperers think he was dead? After all, their voices did sound a little scared. Serve them right to think they had been the cause. And what if he did say something to let them know he was still alive? Might they not just decide to go on teasing him about his ruffled nightshirt? Well, he would not give them the chance to do that!

But how hard it was to hold his tongue when he so desperately wanted to talk to someone! Anyone! He had to clench his teeth together and dig his face into his knees in order to keep silent.

"See, Marty? Not a peep. Flippin' dead, that's wot he is."

"He ain't!" There was a note of desperation in the whispered voice. "I'm tellin' ye he ain't! Sssst! Sssst! Jed, come on. Say somethin'. *Please!*"

"Aw, it's no use, Marty. Come on. We best get back to bed 'fore we get caught."

"Sure an' I guess yer right, Noah. He really is flippin' dead. Aw, the devil take it, anyway. Let's be goin'."

So they were leaving. Colley's only connection to anything human would be gone, leaving him alone in that terrible black hole in the ground. Was not any connection, bad as it might turn out to be, better than none at this moment?

"I ... I ... I'm *not* dead!" Colley could only hope that the small quavering squeak sounded brave and unafraid. Let them see that a ruffled nightshirt did not mean they were dealing with a sissy!

His announcement was first greeted with silence. Then he heard an excited whisper.

"There, told ye so! He ain't dead! Was . . . was that yerself, Jed?"

"Y-y-yes," replied Colley.

"Look, if yer fingers ain't too froze, climb up the ladder so yer closer. Better chance of no one hearin' us. It's me here, Marty, with Noah."

Colley's legs by now were so cramped it was a struggle to stand up. But he somehow managed it and began to crawl up the ladder. He had to accomplish this in total darkness, although when he neared the top of the ladder he saw that there was the faint glow of a lantern, so faint, however, as to be almost non-existent.

"Sorry we got to keep the lantern so low," Marty said. "Soup ain't never yet come 'round after he checks out we're all abed, but nothin' certain in this world. Anyways, I . . . I only wanted ye should know I never meant for the flippin' penny to land where it did, close to yerself as me."

"That's the truth," Noah broke in. "He never did. Marty don't tell lies."

"An' I would o' spoke up, only yerself went and done it first," said Marty.

"He would o' too," said Noah. "Marty don't tell lies."

"Once ye opened yer chops and Mr. Toad Face had it fixed in his froggy brain yerself was the owner," Marty went right on, "I could o' bleated me head off like a flippin' sheep, and it wouldn't o' done no good. But it should o' been *me* in the hole. Why'd ye go an' do it, Jed?"

Colley hesitated. This whole conversation was so unexpected and startling, it was hard for him to get his wits together and remember why he actually *had* done it. "I . . . I thought the penny might be nearer me than you. And . . . and . . . and it didn't much matter for I'm going to die anyway. I know that I am." And that explanation was exactly the truth, for Colley did not tell lies either.

But it was met by an explosion from Marty. "No! No! No! Ye ain't goin' to flippin' die! Ye hear me, Jed? Ye ain't! Meself and me Irish saints are goin' to see to it that ye ain't."

"Wh-wh-why?" asked the disbelieving Colley. After all, he was still finding it difficult to accept that the matter of the ruffled nightshirt had not been brought up.

"I got me reasons," replied Marty. "An' ye might as well know I ain't proud o' how mean we been. None o' us is."

"That's right," piped up Noah. "Marty don't tell lies."

"Ye just make certain yerself stays alive t'night, Jed," Marty said fiercely. "Ain't likely Mr. Toad Face'll keep ye here past mornin'. Then 'rangements got to be made. Not much, but somethin'. Sure an' I'll see to it."

"That's right, he will," said the ever ready Noah. "Marty don't tell—oof!"

It seemed that a sharp dig in the ribs might have taken place with an elbow, courtesy of its owner who wished no more mention made of his good character. Enough, after all, was enough.

"Now, stick yer hand up, Jed," Marty said. "Ye ain't put away enough for a bedbug since ye been here. Put this in yer pocket." He shoved something through the grate. "It's a gummy bun. Ain't important where it come from. But we got to go now. See ye in the mornin'. 'Night, Jed!"

"'Night, Jed," echoed Noah.

Their feet made no more sound than cats' paws as they padded away, leaving Colley alone and in darkness again. Alone to think about what had just happened, and then find it hard to believe it had happened at all. But it seemed as if he might now have two friends in the Broggin Home for Boys. Oh yes, and a gummy bun in his pocket! Then suddenly it was all too much for him. Halfway down the ladder, he stopped to put his head against a rung as tears welled up in his eyes, spilling over and rolling down his cheeks in great, scalding drops.

And it was then he heard the sound again and saw the faint lantern light overhead.

Sssst! Sssst!

The boys must have returned. He could not imagine why, but one thing he knew. They must not know he had been crying. They must not! So he could not answer lest they tell it from his voice. He would just stand there holding his breath and saying nothing. Perhaps they would give up and go away.

Sssst! Sssst!

"Hey, Jed! Come on an' answer. We know yer there."

Sssst! Sssst!

Sssst! Sssst!

Then came the whispers.

"Maybe now he *is* dead, actual."

"Couldn't o' died so soon."

"Maybe he's escaped."

"Don't be a jackass. Escaped how?"

"I dunno."

Sssst! Sssst!

"Hey, say somethin'. You there, Jed?"

Colley could stand this no longer. "Y-y-yes!" he burst out. And to his horror, the word had come in a choking, telltale sob!

There were more whispers, while Colley waited to hear the worst—something said about sissy tears, all connected to the dread, sissy ruffled nightshirt.

"He's been cryin'."

"So what if he has? He has a right, don't he? We all done it one time or 'nother. An' who's to blame him?"

"I ain't blamin' him!"

"An' you ain't to say nothin' 'bout it neither. None o' us is. Marty wouldn't like it."

Marty would not like it? Then these whispered voices were not those of Marty and Noah? Who then?

"Jed? Jed, this here's Toby. I come to say I'm sorry I were mean 'long with the rest. Ain't yer fault yer here, no more'n any o' us."

"I'm Zack, an' I'm sorry too," another whispered voice broke in.

"Me too," came another eager whisper. "I'm Rufus. An' . . . an' if you was wearin' ruffles where you come from, then comin' here's worse for you nor any o' the rest o' us."

"I ain't even *seed* a nightshirt with ruffles afore," said Toby.

"See here," Zack jumped in. "We wasn't supposed to say nothin' 'bout them ruffles. Now look what you gone and done. Marty ain't goin' to like it."

"Aw, I never meant nothin'," said Rufus. "An' you don't got to tell on me, Zack."

A long silence followed this exchange as if, having made a mess of the confession, no one quite knew what was to be said next. Of course, with all this eagerness to confess a wrongdoing, Colley had hardly had a chance to put in a word edgewise. But now he felt he ought to say *something*.

"It's all right, really it is. And anyway, I don't even have the ruffles anymore. I have a nightshirt like all . . . all the rest of you now."

"So you do," said Rufus. Even in the darkness, it was almost possible to imagine the smile creasing his sallow face.

"Well, see you in the mornin'. 'Night, Jed," Toby said.

"'Night, Jed," said Rufus.

"'Night, Jed," said Zack.

"Good . . . good night, everyone," said Colley. "See . . . see you in the morning."

As soon as he was certain the boys had left, Colley scrambled back down the ladder. His tears were all dried up by now, and he did not think they would be back. He dropped down onto the stone floor, crossed his legs, fished the gummy bun from his pocket, and took a big bite from it. It made no difference at all to him that he had not been told where it came from. All that mattered to him was that though he was sitting alone in the dark in a deep hole in the ground at the very bottom of the Broggin Home for Boys, he was enjoying one of the best meals he had ever had in his life!

Chapter X

A Frightening Fall

Eeeek!

The rusty hinges squealed, and the iron grate fell back on the stone floor with a shattering crash. Awakened with a start from the sleep that had finally overtaken him, Colley looked up to see the grate open and a lantern light flicker eerily over something a deadly, flabby white. It was the chin of Mr. Crawler, whose squat face was peering down the hole.

"Hey you, down there! You get on up here!" That the voice had more the sound of a snarling dog than the expected croak of a swamp toad meant little to the cowering figure at the bottom of the hole. All that mattered was that it issued from the ugly throat of Mr. Crawler, and must be obeyed at once.

Colley had not believed he could hurt or ache more than after a day at the glass factory, but a night spent curled up into a cramped, shivering ball at the bottom of a hole in the ground proved him wrong. He dragged himself painfully to his feet, and was barely able to make it to the top of the ladder.

He had no sooner arrived there than he was snatched out of the hole by the collar, hauled down the cellar hall like the morning's garbage collection, and thrown into the cellar room by a Mr.

Crawler whose mouth was so tightly compressed in his vast, flabby chin that there appeared to be no mouth at all. This sign of his fury was evidence to the fact that the criminal Colley was now being held guilty of two crimes, the first, that of pocketing a penny he should have turned over to his benevolent benefactors, and the second, being responsible for Mr. Crawler's losing several valuable minutes of sleep on his behalf.

In the room the lanterns had already been lit, and the five boys, yawning and rubbing their eyes, had climbed from their cots and were pulling off their nightshirts. But when Colley came hurtling into the room, every boy stopped what he was doing to give him a wide, friendly, sleepy grin.

"Mornin', Jed!"

"Mornin', Jed!"

"Mornin', Jed!"

"Mornin', Jed!"

"Mornin', Jed!"

"G-good morning!" said Colley, feeling strangely shy as he crossed the room. Having never changed into his nightshirt the evening before, he had nothing to do now except sit perched on the edge of his cot to wait until time to leave the room. Curled up on the floor of the hole, he had almost begun to think he had dreamed the boys' visits. He was still finding it almost impossible to believe. What could have happened to make them treat him so differently? Was it only that he no longer had his ruffled nightshirt? That did not seem like much of a reason, but he could think of nothing else. All he hoped was that they were not just teasing him.

"Jed! Jed! Come on! We'll be late!" Marty called out. Lantern in hand, he was standing in the doorway.

And so were Noah and Rufus and Toby and Zack. Lost in his thoughts, he had not noticed that they were all ready and gathered at the door, clearly waiting for him. For *him,* Colley! Quickly he climbed to his feet, but his legs were still so cramped from his night spent in the hole that he tottered as he started down the room. Marty instantly ran up to him.

"Ye all right, Jed? Sure an' bein' in that flippin' hole all night ain't no picnic. *We* know! Ye think as how ye can make it?"

Colley nodded. "Yes, I . . . I can. Th-thank you."

"All right then," Marty said. "But see here, Jed, ye got to get down yer porridge. Ye don't, and ye ain't never goin' to live the day out. One gummy bun ain't goin' to make it for anyone in glass works, nor any place they put ye to work 'round here. But 'specially glass works."

"Ain't *them* the truest words ever spoke!" Toby blurted.

"But they won't give me anything more," Colley said. "I still have something left in my bowl."

Marty snorted. "I know. I seen. One flippin' lump hard as a murderin' stone by now's my guess. But ye'll be findin' more in yer bowl today. I . . . I been makin' 'rangements."

"An' he done it if he says so," Noah said, bobbing his head. "Marty don't tell lies."

Marty gave no sign of even having heard this. "Just see yerself eats any pickin' thing what ye get, Jed," he said. "Shove it down no matter what. But don't go runnin' nowhere once we been to the facilities. Don't go for yer porridge till ye seen me first. Right now, I got to talk to someone. Ye lot, watch out for him!"

With that, Marty raced off down the hall and up the stairs, disappearing through the door that led to the yard. Colley hurried along with the other boys, or at least tried to hurry. His legs were still stiff, and he was barely able to control them. As he climbed the first step up, he stumbled and started to catapult forward. Faster than any eye could blink, hands darted out from either side of him, and each of his arms was grabbed by a set of wiry fingers, one belonging to Noah, the other to Zack. Until they reached the top of the stairs and started through the door, the boys' fingers remained tightly gripped around his arms.

In the yard they joined up with a line of boys all yawning and shivering, with arms wrapped around themselves and dancing about to protect themselves against the early morning cold as they awaited their turn. Colley saw at once that Marty was not in the same line, but he had joined up with another, where he was holding a whispered conference with Silas, Colley's partner in the scullery. They appeared to be casting secret glances in Colley's direction, which gave him a sinking feeling in his stomach. After all, it had only been a few hours since he had been an outcast. And what could Marty be having to say about him, if indeed he were the subject of the conversation, except to poke fun at him? Besides, Colley was used to being teased and turned upon. It had happened so often he almost expected it. So when Marty joined them back in the building, Colley could only look at him warily.

Then the first thing Marty said was, "Put out the hand ye eat with, Jed."

To do what with? Grab it and twist it as Duncan had once done? Or put a spider in it, a trick Hugo had thought so clever? Colley did not put out his hand, or even move.

"Come on," said Marty impatiently. "Sure an' I ain't goin' to bite it."

Colley looked around him and saw all the boys grinning. Well, let them! He would take whatever was handed him, and no matter what it was, he would laugh at it. There would be no more Mister Sissy Ruffles! Boldly, or so he hoped it appeared, he stuck out his hand.

Marty then immediately pulled from his pants pocket a small, brown-paper packet, opened it, and poured the contents into Colley's outstretched hand.

It looked like . . . it felt like . . . could it be?

"S-s-sugar?" stammered Colley. "Is it sugar?"

Marty grinned. "Ain't nothin' else."

"An' Marty don't tell lies!" said Noah, as the grins on the faces around him widened.

"But ye ain't to go eatin' it, not now anyways," Marty said. "Wot ye got to do is curl yer fingers 'round it like such." He demonstrated by making his hand into a fist.

Colley did as told. "Like that?"

Marty nodded. "Now ye keep yer fingers like that all the way till Soup gives ye yer porridge. Then, 'fore ye pick up yer cup, ye fly yer hand over the porridge, open up yer fingers just 'nough to let out the sugar. It ain't much, Jed, but 'nough to help ye get started on gettin' the stuff down."

"Oh, thank you!" said Colley. "But won't Mr. and Mrs. Crawley see what I'm doing? What if I'm not clever enough and they catch me?"

"Ye'll do it," Marty said matter-of-factly. "We all done it one time or 'nother. They didn't catch none o' us."

"Nary a one," said Noah proudly.

"But what if Soup doesn't give me any fresh porridge?" Colley asked.

"*He* will," said Marty, his face expressionless. "I made 'rangements."

And Marty had indeed, for when Colley held out his hand for his bowl, it was filled with hot porridge. How Marty had made the "'rangement" with Soup, Colley had no idea. But now was not the time to think about it. His heart lodged in his throat, he had to give every bit of attention to keeping his hand from trembling dangerously as he took the bowl with one hand, passed the other over it, letting the sugar fall over the porridge.

"Did he finish the other?" the sharp voice of Mrs. Crawler cut through the room.

The bowl shook violently in Colley's hand. Bowl, porridge, *and* sugar almost went crashing to the floor. From behind Colley could be heard the collective sucking in of five breaths.

"A-a-appeared that he did, Mrs. Crawler," said Soup, who mercifully stood just far enough away from them so they could not note his face turning as pale as the porridge.

"Hmmmmph!" sniffed Mrs. Crawler, narrowing her eyes and turning to Mr. Crawler with tightened lips to obtain a second opinion.

"Get to your seat then!" snarled Mr. Crawler after a few moments spent in deciding, no doubt, if it were worth his trouble to go digging into a bowl of sticky porridge to see if a hard lump still remained from a previous meal. He decided to content himself with merely glaring at Colley as he made his shaky way to his place at the table.

There was no doubt that the sugar helped Colley get down the porridge, even though not three days earlier it was something he would have sent back to the kitchen at Trevelyan House in disgust. Something else, however, helped get down the porridge as well. That was an under-the-table dig in the ribs made by Marty's elbow. Though the expression on Marty's face never changed as he dug into his own porridge, Colley knew what the dig in the ribs meant. It was Marty saying, "There, told ye so. Sure an' didn't I know ye could do it?" And this under the four sets of Obadiah and Quintilla Crawler eyes!

There was also no question about the benefits of a stomach full of hot porridge, no matter what the quality, over one so empty that, excepting the earlier presence of one small gummy bun, it was shrunk almost to the backbone. If only the porridge proved enough to help keep Colley going at the glass works.

Any hopes he had in that direction, however, soon evaporated when he walked through the door and was struck by the noise, the fumes, and murdering heat pouring out from the furnaces. Even with food now in his stomach, and knowing he had friends at the Broggin Home for Boys, how many days could he survive such a place?

Days? Why, by early afternoon, he did not think he could last even that day. As he made his way to the cooling oven, his throat parched and his eyes burning, precariously balancing three red-hot bottles on a big, clumsy shovel, he felt his legs wobbling frighteningly under him. He knew he was not keeping up the slow run expected of the carrying-in boys and felt certain that as he passed Gorp, he was being narrowly watched. Then suddenly, without warning, he felt himself lurching forward. There was no way to stop himself, and he knew he was going to fall right on top of the scorching bottles, or perhaps worse, up against one of the searing hot ovens.

But as it turned out, neither of these things happened. For just as had happened earlier that day, a set of wiry fingers clamped themselves like manacles around one of his arms, pulling him back upright again. The fingers belonged to Silas.

"Hey, what do you think you're doin'?" Gorp snarled.

"Jed was 'bout to go fallin' right atop of . . ." Silas began quickly.

"Well, never you mind what he was goin' to go fallin' atop of," snapped Gorp. "Anyone 'round this place makes mistakes, they got to pay for 'em. Only way lessons get learned. But what Jed does ain't none o' your business. You got that, Broggin boy?"

Silas bit his lip so hard it turned white. "Yes, sir, Mr. Gorp," he said, his eyes fastened tightly on Gorp's boots.

"All right then, don't you go forgittin' it. Now both o' you git back to work!" With a last ugly look over his shoulder, Gorp stomped off.

"Th-thank you, Silas," Colley said under his breath.

"Weren't nothin'," Silas muttered, adding in an embarrassed manner, "Marty said I should look out for you." He turned on his heels to leave, but then hesitated, and turned back again, looking nervously over his shoulder in Gorp's direction. "But keep an eye out for yer back, Jed. Keep a sharp eye!" Then, breaking into a dogtrot, he ran off without looking back again.

"Keep a sharp eye out for yer back, Jed. Keep a sharp eye!"

For what?

For whom?

And again the same question—*why?*

Chapter XI

A Surprising Revelation

Sssst! Sssst!

At the sound coming through the darkness, Colley's heart began to beat faster. This time he knew what it meant. It was a signal from the boys in his room that he was soon to have something important revealed to him. It was, he felt, the final sign that he really was now one of them.

It was to be a "grand surprise," Marty had said. Colley suspected it had something to do with the boys' disappearance under the cot, and the surprise was a tunnel, a cold, dank, dark tunnel. But Colley had no intention of spoiling it for them. If he had to, he would pretend to be just as surprised and pleased as it was possible to be.

Sssst! Sssst!

"Come on, Jed!" Marty's whispered voice was accompanied by the squeak of springs and the sound of his feet thumping down on the floor. "Soup's been and gone. It's safe now. Ye didn't go an' drop off to sleep, did ye?"

"Oh no! I'm coming!" Colley whispered back. Drop off to sleep indeed! His heart was racing as he tiptoed toward the tiny lantern light that flared up in the middle of the room. After all, this was the first time Colley had ever had a secret shared with him by boys he knew.

"Sure an' we're pleased ye could make it, Jed," Marty said. "Anyways, now we're all here, somebody get the cover. All of ye go on, and meself will wait here with Jed."

"I'll get it," Zack said at once, quickly dropping down and reaching under the cot.

There followed the same scraping sound Colley remembered, and then Zack reached up a hand. "Give it here, Tobe."

Toby handed him the lantern, which flared even brighter as Zack turned it up and crawled with it under the cot. The other boys scrambled after him, and then Marty gave him a little push. "Yerself can follow 'em, Jed. But ye'll be climbin' down a ladder, so watch out."

Colley ducked down at once and crawled under the cot toward the glow of the lantern shining from a hole in the floor. Peering down the hole, he saw a rough wooden ladder and started down it, with Marty coming down directly behind him. As soon as Marty's head cleared the top, he reached up and dragged the square, splintered wood cover back over the hole before following Colley down. The other boys all stood pressed together at the foot of the ladder, staring intently at Colley as he turned to face them.

Then to the delight of all of them, Toby, Zack, Noah, Rufus, and Marty—if their wide grins were any evidence of it—Colley gasped and his eyes flew wide open. For though he did indeed find himself in a tunnel just as he had suspected he would, how different the scene was from what he had imagined it to be. He hardly needed to pretend to be surprised. He *was* surprised!

The tunnel, at least for a short distance, was cheerfully lit not only by the lantern brought down by Zack, but by two others as well, set on the floor. And what the light revealed was a cozy scene featuring two pieces of carpet circled by two chairs and four wood boxes. Against a wall stood a cupboard made up of boxes, one piled atop the other to form shelves on which were stacked an assortment of cups and plates. There were even pictures decorating the walls, almost too many to count.

It made no difference to Colley, and in truth he hardly noticed, that the carpet pieces were little more than rags, so worn, frayed, and moth-eaten that the few bits of red, gold, and blue wool barely revealed that they might once have made up a pattern. And it made no difference either that the chairs were little wood skeletons with spindles missing on the backs, and paint-chipped legs that needed to be supported by what appeared to be large chunks of jagged stone. Nor did Colley care that all the rough, splintered boxes bore torn labels announcing that they had once been the containers of cabbages, potatoes, and turnips. He did not care further that not one cup or dish on the shelf, outside of being badly chipped or cracked, bore the slightest resemblance to any other, or that the pictures on the walls were nothing but crumpled, dirty bits and pieces of paper barely recognizable as pictures.

"Sure an' welcome to our home, Jed," Marty said, beaming.

"It's somethin', ain't it?" said Noah, his skinny, sunken chest visibly swelling with pride.

"What do you think, Jed?" Rufus asked eagerly.

Zack's pale eyebrows drew together over his washed-out eyes in a worried frown. "Ain't you got nothin' to say, Jed?"

"Oh . . . oh, *yes!*" breathed Colley. "I . . . I think it's . . . it's . . ."

"Poifect?" Toby suggested hesitantly.

"Yes!" said Colley. "That's exactly what it is!"

Toby produced a chip-toothed grin and dug Rufus in the ribs with an elbow. "Here that, Rufe? Jed thinks as how it's poifect!"

"We figgered as how ye'd like it, Jed," said Marty, as all the boys stood there grinning and elbowing each other in the ribs.

Then, suddenly, Noah broke away from the others and ran to the wall behind him. "Look, Jed, look!" He pointed to the wall, hopping from one foot to the other with pent-up excitement.

"This here's one *I* found. It's the picter of a real ship. See? See?"

Zack's pale, sad eyes came to life as he ran up beside Noah. "An' this is one *I* got. It's of a dog, and under is numbers wot says wot day it is."

A moment later Toby, Rufus, and Marty were all just as eagerly pointing out to Colley the pictures each had found, some from calendars, some pages torn from magazines, and some parts of posters torn from lampposts and billboards.

Colley examined each one carefully. "Where did you ever find them all?" he asked.

"Rubbish heaps, mostly," Marty replied. "Some garbage pails."

"I found the ship picter blowin' down the gutter. Saved it just 'fore it were 'bout to go down the sewer," said Noah proudly.

"But . . . but how did you ever get them in here?" asked Colley, the dreaded word "pocket" still fresh in his memory.

"Aw, picters is easy, ain't they, Marty?" Rufus said.

"Nothin' much to it, if yer brains ain't gone an' run out yer ears," replied Marty. "Find 'em goin' to and from work an' just stick 'em inside yer trousers. But meself knows wot yer thinkin', Jed, and it's 'bout Mr. Toad Face an' them pockets. Well, even if we got caught with picters, wouldn't make no difference. They ain't worth nothin'. But that flippin' penny! I should o' swallowed it!"

"Yeah!" the others all agreed, heads nodding.

"What about the rest?" Colley asked. "However did you manage all that?"

"Boxes wasn't too hard neither," Noah said. "Ain't that right, Marty?"

Marty nodded. "Boiler uses them kinds o' boxes to bring stuff back from the market."

"Not always just the market neither," Rufus said. "Most o' the times he picks up stuff from wherever he sees somethin' he figgers pigs would be willin' to eat. An' if pigs is willin', then boys oughter be willin'."

"Sure an' ain't that the bitter truth," said Marty, screwing up his nose. "Anyways, where he keeps them boxes is in the coal room. He got so many piled up in there, he don't know how many. Most nights he's dead out cold, snorin' up a storm, so we just tippy-toes on in and borries some. He don't remember 'nough in the mornin' to spit in yer eye. An' one box missin' now an' again, he don't know no difference."

Zack snickered. "Wonder is he finds his way home nights."

The boys all nodded their cheerful agreement to this observation.

"Now tell Jed 'bout the chairs and rugs," Toby said.

"Tobe, ye was the one wot found 'em," said Marty. "So ye tell Jed."

"Aw, weren't much," said Toby bashfully, studying his toes. "I just found 'em all piled up back o' the furnace when I were shovelin' coal. Looked just like a heap o' sticks and rags."

"But they wasn't, Tobe," Rufus said. "An' you was smart to see it."

"Aw, weren't nothin'," said Toby, returning to the study of his toes.

"Were too," said Rufus. "An' all we needed for them chairs was somethin' to hold 'em up, an' we found that in . . ."

"Maybe we better wait an' tell Jed 'bout that later, Rufe," Marty broke in quickly. "I seen him yawnin' an' yawnin', an' he got to get back to bed. We all do, but we ain't none o' us in glass works now, an' glass works is hard 'nough, never mind no sleep atop o' it."

"But I seen how he ate better at supper, Marty," Noah said.

"Faith an' that he did," replied Marty.

"An' it weren't one o' Boiler's best neither, it bein' nothin' but cabbage leafs and 'taters," Rufus added.

"Boiler's best!" Toby shook his head and sighed. "Boiler ain't got no best, Rufe."

"Well, sometimes there's meat," Rufus said.

"Meat!" snorted Zack. "Anybody'd think you ain't never seen

wot Boiler brings in them boxes. Wot gets dropped and swept off'n the butcher's floor ain't my idea o' meat."

"*Smells* like meat, anyhow," persisted Rufus. "An' alongside o' that, Zack, any stuff wot goes in the pot that ain't supposed to be there, or ain't quite dead, gets boiled dead."

"C'mon, all o' ye," Marty broke in. "Jed here's just gettin' round to eatin' and ye go and make it so he won't be able to no more, listenin' to ye goin' on."

"Oh, it's all right," Colley said at once, although in truth such a description of what he *would* be eating came close to causing what he had *already* eaten to come pouring right back up again! "I . . .I must get used to it."

"Naw, it ain't all right," Marty said. "It ain't all right to be hearin' 'bout it in a heap with no warnin'. Food here's bad 'nough to make a roach croak, that's the flippin' truth. But see, it ain't no worse'n what we was all eatin' most times 'fore we was brung here."

"An' don't forget, Marty, they was times when we was eatin' nothin'," Noah said.

"Sure an' don't I know it," Marty muttered. "But right now what we come for, 'sides interdoocin' ye to our home, Jed, is 'cause we got somethin' to tell 'bout when yerself first come here. It ain't right ye shouldn't know. An' it's somethin' wot I did, so I'll tell it."

"Aw, we all did it, Marty," said Rufus. "Didn't we?" He looked around at Noah, Zack, and Toby, who all nodded their agreement.

"But 'twas meself started it," said Marty. "'Twas meself made ye do wot ye done. Anyways, help yerself to a seat, Jed." Marty pointed to one of the two chairs.

As Colley sat down carefully on one of the chairs precariously balanced on a jagged piece of stone, Marty and the other boys all found places on the remaining chair and the boxes. Then, the tunnel fell silent and still as, with all eyes fastened on Marty, everyone waited for him to begin his confession.

Chapter XII

A Confession

For a long while nothing moved in the tunnel room but the shadows cast by the fluttering lantern lights. Marty sat staring at the ragged bit of carpet under his feet. It was clear that he was finding it difficult to begin his speech.

Then at last it was Noah who blurted, "They was a Jed afore you, an' he were Marty's friend. They was together in glass works."

This pronouncement brought Marty quickly to life. "Thank ye, Noah, but I'm able to tell it now," he said. "But wot Noah says is true, Jed. They was a Jed just afore ye. We was on the streets an' got brung in the same time. Jed weren't his real name no more'n any o' us got real names, but Jed were the name wot were give him, an' he got put in the cot next to meself."

"My . . . my cot?" asked Colley softly.

"Sure an' it were the very same one," Marty replied. "An' it's like Noah said, we got put in glass works together. But then lucky meself got pulled out an' put in the mills 'longside o' Noah an' Toby an' Rufus an' Zack. Mills ain't like goin' to heaven, but better'n glass works anyways ye figger it. We went on hopin' as how Jed would likewise get pulled out, but he just stayed on and in glass works. Then he got some kind o' lung sickness. He got sicker an'

77

sicker, but them Crawlers never give him no medicine nor nothin' and went on sendin' him back to work. An' then one day he just never turned up for dinner. Nobody told us nothin', but then Silas said as how he were carried out dead from the glass works. We never seen him again." Marty hesitated, for his voice had started to quaver dangerously.

"An' that's the livin' truth, Jed," said Noah, coming to his friend's rescue. "Marty don't tell lies."

Marty just shrugged. "Never had no notion how come 'twas meself got pulled out o' glass works till Soup told me. He'd heard say it were 'cause o' me honest face. Ain't that the flippin' somethin'?"

"You *do* have a honest face, Marty," said Noah. "Ain't I always sayin' . . ."

Marty quickly stopped him. "Wot *yer* sayin' is one thing, Noah. But who cares when it gets said by them slippery lawyer gents wot comes 'round here rubbin' their slimy hands an' sayin' 'Just fine! Just fine!', lyin' to them pretty young ladies who thinks as how wot they're doin' is good works, givin' money for the boys in the Broggin Home so's they'll get proper food an' a edication. Wot a flippin' joke! But seems wot them gents wanted were a boy to help Soup cleanin' up their rooms, which is nearby the mills, so meself an' me honest face gets chose. Jed had a honest face too, but wot he never had was no bleedin' luck!"

"But that weren't yer fault, Marty," Toby said. "It weren't."

"I know," Marty said, "an' it's wot meself keeps tellin' meself. But thank ye for it, Tobe. Anyways, not too far later, ye come 'long, Jed, and they give ye the name. Made me mad, an' that's the burnin' truth. Made me so mad I never stopped to think as how it weren't yer fault. An' it weren't right for us to make fun o' yer nightshirt. Them ruffles weren't yer fault neither, nor how ye talk different from the rest o' us. I knowed it were wrong doin' wot we was doin', an' meself leadin' the way."

"Ain't nowhere it said us got to do every flippin' thing wot you do, Marty," Toby said. "Maybe we just wanted to. So it weren't all yer fault."

"Not all, but it were plenty, Tobe," Marty said. "Anyways, after ye 'fessed up to that murderin' penny, Jed, we all talked an' said how wrong it were in us to be treatin' ye the way we was. Yer different from all o' us, an' that's the flippin' truth, but that don't make ye bad."

"An' don't forget wot else, Marty," Rufus broke in eagerly. "We all said as how it must o' been a hunerd times harder for you, Jed, than it were for us. We ain't so stoopid as to see how you ain't from the streets like the rest o' us."

"An' gettin' put in glass works!" exclaimed Toby, just as eagerly. "Glass works is the worse."

"An' gettin' scullery very first night!" said Zack, shaking his head in disbelief. "Very first night!"

"An' we was all o' one mind, wasn't we, how Jed must o' had someone wot took care o' him proper and cared 'bout him. Not like all o' us," Noah said, finally having his turn at a confession that was going considerably better than the one they had when Colley was imprisoned in the hole. "Tell Jed 'bout them birds yer always talkin' 'bout, Marty."

"Aw, it ain't nothin' much," Marty replied, squirming uncomfortably.

"'Tis, too," Noah insisted. "Tell it, Marty."

Marty hesitated a moment, his eyes growing distant. "Sure an' it's just that we're like them sparrows that fly 'bout in the sky. All them millions and millions o' sparrows just floatin' 'round. There's so many o' them birds, nobody counts. So when one o' them falls from the sky, nobody cares, 'cause 'nother one comes an' fills up his place so smooth they ain't a mark left where t'other one been. An' no more notice is give o' us than them birds. If one o' us drops dead in glass works or the mills or even in the flippin' scullery, who do we got to know or care?"

"You . . . you have each other," Colley said simply.

From the looks on the boys' faces, it almost seemed that no one had ever had this thought before. Then, one by one, the fluttering lanterns lit up their smiles.

"Ain't no mistake, we do that!" Marty said, speaking for them all.

"And . . . and didn't you all care about Jed?" Colley asked.

"Faith an' we did!" said Marty. "Yer right."

Then, before he could stop himself, Colley suddenly blurted, "I . . . I never had any friends."

Marty's eyes widened. "*None?*"

Colley shook his head. "I did have some boys who played with me sometimes, but . . . but they were never my friends."

"Sure an' ye got friends now, Jed," Marty said. He looked around at the others. "Ain't he?"

The boys nodded with such ferocity it seemed their heads would fall off their thin shoulders.

Colley had to fight back the tears that sprang suddenly to his eyes. "Th-thank you," he said, swallowing hard. "But . . . about having someone taking care of me and caring for me, that was my mother and father, and . . . and they've just died. Now there's no one left to take care of me but the . . ." Colley stopped, for he had been about to say "servants" and "my tutor," but thought better of it. "I mean my uncle and aunt. They'll have to take care of me once I get ransomed even though they don't care much about me."

"What's 'ransomed' mean, Jed?" Rufus asked.

"Means somebody pays money to get you back, don't it?" said Toby.

Zack threw a hand to his forehead as his jaw fell. "You mean somebody's goin' to pay money to get you back to take care o' you? Where'd you get a notion like that?"

"Do ye know wot yer sayin', Jed?" Marty asked.

"I think so," replied Colley. "It's something I've thought from the beginning when I was kidnapped and brought here. Then when Mr. and Mrs. Crawler were talking, I remember they said something about . . . I think it was 'terms of the transaction.' I believe it had to do with getting money for me."

"Jed," Marty said gently, "we ain't never used a word like 'kidnapped' like ye just done, but we was *all* picked up an' brung here with nary a by-yer-leave. So seems more nor less as we was all kidnapped too. An' they was them other things, them 'terms' too for each o' us. Wot that means is Mr. Toad Face paid for ye like he did for all o' us, meself as well. That's the only place where payin' comes in. Sure an' I don't like tellin' it to ye, Jed, but it's the bleedin' truth. It's wot meself were telled."

"He *were* telled that," Noah said. "An' Marty don't tell lies, ain't that so?"

"It's so," chorused Toby, Zack, and Rufus.

Colley felt as if a stone had been dropped into the pit of his stomach. "Who . . . who told you?" he asked.

"Soup were the one wot telled me," replied Marty. "He seen it all writ down in a black book with red goin' down the side somewhere in the toad's hole, that bein' the room where Mr. Toad Face an' his charmin' madam gives greetin's to their new wictims. Soup seen his own name in it, an' seen where he never fetched much to the person wot brung him in. Soup said he weren't surprised, wot with his kind o' leg and back."

"Marty says Soup knows he ain't good for much," Rufus broke in. "Thinks he's lucky they give him a job here. He thinks them Crawlers done him a favor. Ain't that right, Marty?"

"It's right, Rufe," Marty said. "But murderin' snakes, Jed, did ye really think as how someone were soon goin' to be payin' money to get ye out o' here?"

Yes, he did, but now all hope for that was gone. Stunned from this terrible revelation, Colley could do no more than nod his head.

"All o' us is sorry 'bout it, Jed," Marty said. "But ain't nothin' any o' us can do 'bout it."

"I know," Colley said. "And I had to learn about it sometime. It's just that . . . that I thought perhaps I might be able to keep alive until then, if it wasn't too long from now."

"Ye see here, Jed," Marty said fiercely, "don't ye 'member wot I said to ye when ye were in the hole? It were that meself and me Irish saints were goin' to see that ye ain't goin' to die. I lost meself one Jed, an' I ain't goin' to lose meself another. Wot ye got to do is eat yer tomfool head off like the other Jed never would. Never mind wot were said 'bout the food. Ye just got to eat."

"An' never forget drinkin', Marty," Toby said. "'Member wot you said 'bout that? You said when you was in glass works, you just kep' goin' an' goin' to the spigot till you thought as you was goin' to bust open. You said it were wot kep' you livin'."

"Sure an' it did," Marty said. "Just drink an' drink till yer eyeballs pop. Silas'll give ye a poke now an' again to see ye do it. Silas were me friend when I were in glass works, an' meself asked him to look out for ye."

"He already has looked out for me, Marty," Colley said. "He helped me up when I fell this morning."

"Ye ain't said nothin' 'bout fallin'," Marty replied quickly. "How'd it happen?"

"I just tumbled," explained Colley. "One thing odd, though, was after Silas helped me up and was running off, he said I should keep a sharp eye out for my back. I don't know what he meant by that. Do you?"

Marty scratched an ear, thinking this over. "I ain't talked to Silas yet, but I'll find out 'bout it. Anyways, one thing's for sure, ye ain't goin' to die, not in this place leastways. Yer goin' to keep right on livin' an' joinin' the rest o' us when we go runnin' 'way from here."

"An' go to sea!" added Noah excitedly. "All o' us on the same ship just like the one in my picter."

"But only soon as ever we're old 'nough," Rufus said.

"Else we'd just get picked up an' brung right back here," Toby concluded with a rueful shake of his head.

"Or get sent to the mines to be a breaker boy," Zack added woefully. "I hear tell bein' one o' them's worse'n bein' in glass works."

"Sure an' that's the burnin' truth, else I might o' done it when I were in glass works meself," Marty said. "No use runnin' 'way when ye ain't got no place better to run, and the place ye get to might be a whole lot worse."

"Still an' all, nice to know we can run any time we ain't affeared to take a chance," Toby said dreamily.

"Do . . . do you mean you could run away right now if you wanted?" asked Colley in amazement.

"Any ol' time," said Marty airily. "This is a tunnel, ain't it?"

Why yes, indeed it was! And had Colley not lain in his cot two nights earlier thinking that the boys had escaped through that very tunnel, leaving him behind? Now, here he was being invited to join them when they ran off! "But . . . but where does it end?" he asked.

"Why not we just show him?" Rufus asked.

"It's gettin' late, Rufe," Marty replied. "We got to get some sleep, 'specially Jed."

"Aw, it ain't late," said Toby. "No more'n when we wait for one o' us to get back from scullery. Let's show him now."

Zack gave a deep sigh. "Wot if he don't like it?"

"If he don't like it t'night, Zack," said Noah, "waitin' ain't goin' to make him like it no better. C'mon, Marty, we ain't been here a hour."

"Seems as how 'tis up to Jed," Marty said. "How 'bout it, Jed? Ye up to makin' a trip down the tunnel? It ain't a very long one, when ye get down to it."

Colley had already almost stopped noticing his aching bones, his hurting chest, or how tired he was. As for the blow he had received about the ransom, he would think about that later. Right now all that mattered was going down the tunnel with his friends.

"Oh yes," he breathed. "I'd like it!"

"Well then," said Marty, picking up a lantern. "Come on, ye lot, an' let's get goin'."

Moments later, with Marty leading the way swinging the lantern in his hand, they had started down the tunnel.

Chapter XIII

Gravestones

They had gone no more than a few steps when the cozy scene abruptly ended and they entered the tunnel of Colley's imagination, dank mildewed walls and cold, slimy stone underfoot. The only light now came from the one fluttering lantern in Marty's hand, of little more use than the light from a firefly. Further, just as they left the boys' den, they passed what appeared to be a large box hulking against the wall, and from behind it came scratching, scrabbling sounds. Rats? Colley felt goose bumps rising on his skin under his gray flannel nightshirt. Curiously, the other boys appeared quite indifferent to the sound.

"What we're passin' under now's the alley," Marty said.

"Just over our heads is where Boiler brings all them good things for us to eat," said Toby, making some choking, gagging sounds, which were cheerfully picked up on and repeated by Noah, Rufus, and Zack.

"Now," said Marty, "we're passin' under the buildin' right up 'gainst the alley the other side o' the Broggin Home."

After that, they went no more than fifteen or twenty steps before a solid wall rose in front of them. Up the side of it climbed a narrow stairway of rough stone steps.

"But we haven't gone very far," Colley said. "Is this all of the tunnel?"

"It's like I said," Marty replied. "Ain't much o' one. But wot ye really want to see is wot's outside at the top o' them steps. So come on then, an' we'll show ye."

He started up the steps with Colley and the others following after him. When Marty neared the top, he reached up and lifted an old, blackened wood trapdoor a few inches. Peering cautiously through the opening, he lifted it a few inches more. Then he beckoned Colley to come up beside him.

"Ain't we goin' out?" Toby asked.

"No, we ain't, Tobe," Marty said over his shoulder. "Ain't no moon an' darker'n flippin' pitch out there. Ain't worth the risk to take a lantern out. Ye knows that. See, Jed, just outside the tunnel, there's buildin's, which got no windows, all 'round three sides. Last side's a high wall o' brick. Even so, don't seem safe to go out when we ain't got no moon to see by, and we got to take a lantern. 'Pears as how a body seein' a bit o' light dancin' 'round from a lantern might get to wonderin', 'specially comin' from a place like wot's out there. Are ye able to see it, Jed?"

Colley peered through the partially opened trapdoor. Then he peered again, squinting to see what was lit up by the small stream of light coming from the lantern. Then finally, he gasped.

"It . . . it looks like a . . . a graveyard!"

"Faith an' it ain't nothin' else," Marty said matter-of-factly.

"We goes out in it all the time," Noah said, pressing to look over Colley's shoulder.

"But not all o' us at once 'ceptin' late at night," Zack said. "We got to take turns afore dinner when all the rest's still in the yard."

"Zack means the yard, which got the flippin' name o' *play* yard, an' not the graveyard," Rufus explained quickly.

"Reason for takin' turns," Marty said, "is so's we ain't all comin' up missin' the same time. One by one is how we goes."

"What do you do in the graveyard?" Colley whispered.

"Mostly wander 'bout enjoyin' the grass an' a bird maybe wot finds its way in," Marty replied.

"It's all a mess o' weeds," said Toby, poking his head up alongside of Colley. "'Ceptin' for 'roun' the stone each one o' us has chose for hisself. We keeps *them* nice."

"Why did you choose stones?" Colley asked.

"'Cause none o' us got families no more," Marty said. "Wot we done's choose a name on a gravestone an' pertend like it were our own granda or some such. An' that's wot name we takes. Ain't like stealin' or nothin', 'cause nobody comes here, so them names don't belong to nobody."

"An' now Jed can choose one for hisself, ain't that so?" Noah said.

"An' Jed probable can choose one *by* hisself," said Toby. "He ain't goin' to need Zack to read the gravestone for him like all o' us wot don't read so good."

"Ain't we talked 'bout gravestones long 'nough?" came the plaintive voice of Rufus, who had not been able to shove his way to the top and was still standing on a step below the rest. "Wot 'bout eats, Marty? Next yer goin' to say we ain't got no time for 'em."

"Ye got any more questions, Jed?" Marty asked.

"Only one," said Colley. "If there are big buildings all around the graveyard on three sides, and a brick wall on the other, how would you escape?"

"Sure an' there's a wood gate on one side o' the wall. Anyone wot wants can come in. Anyone wot wants can go out. When we gets ready to go, why we'll just take the way out."

"Hasn't anybody ever come into the graveyard while you're there?" Colley asked.

"Not even someone wot's not livin' nor breathin'," said Marty. "Nor anyone else. Here, Rufe, here's the lantern. Ye lead the way back."

The lantern was passed down to Rufus, and then they all pad-padded down the stairs, their bare feet making a soft thumping sound as they went.

As soon as they arrived back at their den, Rufus put down the lantern and ran to the cupboard built of boxes. "I'll get the eats," he announced. "All o' you take a chair."

Colley hurried to the nearest box he could find and thumped down on it as the others dropped onto the seats around him. He wanted to be certain he was not one of the boys on a chair this time, for he had no wish to continue being an honored guest. After all, he was one of *them* now. He had no sooner sat down, however, than he drew his feet up onto the box and gave a sharp gasp. For coming from the darkness into the lantern light, and right into the middle of where they all sat, was an enormous brown rat, so fat it could barely waddle. The boys' faces all broke out in grins when they saw it.

"Which one o' ye let him out?" Marty demanded. He was try-ing to look stern, but not being too successful at it.

"*I* did," confessed Toby at once. "Wot's wrong 'bout doin' it?"

"Aw, nothin' I guess," said Marty. "We just should o' warned Jed is all. Jed, this here's Abigail. He's out pet. Ye can put yer foot down. He won't hurt ye none."

Colley carefully lowered his feet as if he were dropping them into a pot of boiling oil. This, of course, only caused the grins around the room to broaden.

"Where . . . where did he come from?" Colley asked, looking warily at the rat.

"Found him wanderin' 'bout the graveyard, so skinny ye could see his bones," Marty said. "Sure an' he's got a bit o' fat on him now, but he ain't complainin'."

Colley watched nervously as Abigail slowly progressed across the floor and dropped down at Noah's feet.

"How is it you named him Abigail?" Colley asked. "Isn't that a girl's name?"

"Zack were the one wot named him," said Rufus, coming from the cupboard with what looked like two gummy buns and a part of another in his hands. "Got the name off a bit o' gravestone wot he found, one o' them two holdin' up the chairs. Zack, he liked the name, an' Abigail, he don't care. Here, Ab, come an' get it!"

Rufus laid the broken piece of bun on the ground, and Abigail immediately waddled over to it and began to gnaw away. If gummy buns were a big part of his diet, it was easy to see why he had become the size that he was.

"O' course," said Toby, almost as if he had read this last in Colley's mind, "Abigail don't just get gummy buns. We find bits o' cabbage leafs an' such for him too."

"That way, he gets his veg," added Noah, as serious as Toby.

While this conversation was taking place, Rufus had been breaking up the remaining buns into equal pieces and passing them out. Finally, he himself dropped down onto the remaining box.

"This . . . this is a very good bun," Colley said, after taking a bite. "It's even better than the last one." This was not what he really wanted to say. He desperately wanted to make a speech letting the boys know how much he liked all that had happened that night. But talking about the bun was what came out. It sounded like a very lame speech indeed!

"Must be 'cause ye ain't eatin' it in the hole," said Marty. "Mostly ain't no difference one from the other."

"How do you get them?" asked Colley, remembering too late that Marty had not cared to tell him before.

With this question, Noah, Toby, Rufus, and Zack all darted glances at Marty.

"Aw, go on, tell him," Toby said. "Ain't he one o' us now?"

"Sure an' if ye got to know," drawled Marty, "them lawyers wot me an' Soup cleans up behind has got a real sweet tooth for gummy buns an' sugar in their tea. They got piles o' both in a cupboard. Nobody counts, so me and me honest face just pinches wotever I can get inside me shirt. So wot do ye think 'bout that?"

Nothing in the world could have put a stop to the wide grin that crossed Colley's face. Noah, Toby, Rufus, and Zack, licking their sticky fingers, all grinned right back.

It seemed to Colley that he had made just the right speech after all!

Chapter XIV

Education
for the Broggin Boys

The following morning, as the Broggin boys were finishing their porridge, Mr. Crawler stood up and fixed them all with a baleful stare. "You will return to your seats this morning when breakfast is over. We will have school today."

One might have expected that this announcement would result in some change of expression in the pale faces of the boys around the table, but there was none. Not even an eyelash flickered. All Colley could think, however, was that, no matter what was meant by "school," he would have a whole day away from the glass works!

"You and you," snapped Mr. Crawler, shooting out a fat finger at two boys.

The boys elected scrambled from their seats and scurried to the large cupboard against the wall, which was now being unlocked by Soup. Making several trips to the cupboard, the boys dragged out large cardboard boxes that they set in rows down the table. The boxes, when opened, were seen to contain an assortment of such things as beads, colored papers, and wires.

All the boys seemed to know what was to be done with the contents of the boxes, for they went to work at once threading the tiny beads on strings, wrapping and pasting thin strips of green paper around the wires, and tying on small bits of colored paper to form flowers at the end of the wires. Except for the sounds made by the work being done, the room was as silent as ever.

Colley had no idea what his task was supposed to be, but after a very few moments, without even glancing at him or saying a word, Marty slid some wires and green paper strips over in front of him. Watching Marty's nimble fingers, Colley was able very quickly to learn how to twist and paste the paper strips around the wires, forming the stems for the paper flowers.

Mr. Crawler had said they were to have school that day, but this seemed like curious work to be considered school. Perhaps soon they would be changing to something that might require books, paper, and pencils. If only, Colley thought, he could turn and ask Marty about this, but he knew that even exchanging glances was dangerous.

Twisting, twisting. Pasting, pasting. The work soon grew tiresome. The bench was hard, and Colley's fingers became sore. Still, he felt he would rather sit there all day if he had to, twisting and twisting, than return to the glass works. But when they had been working for what might have been several hours, Mr. Crawler once again jumped to his feet.

"Pack up and be quick about it!" he ordered. Then he pointed the same fat finger at the same two boys. "And you clear the tables and bring the books."

In minutes the tables had been swept clean of any sign of the work recently performed on them. Not so much as a tiny bead or scrap of paper remained. The two boys, along with Soup, then returned from the cupboard carrying armloads of assorted books, which they doled out one each to the seated boys.

"Assorted" was indeed the right word for the books. No two in the entire lot matched. The only resemblance they bore to each other was that they were all old, all faded, all stained, and some so tattered at the spines it was a wonder the pages held together. Still, they were books, and Colley wondered why the boys looked at them with such dull, indifferent eyes before turning their attention to Mr. and Mrs. Crawler. This time it was Mrs. Crawler who spoke.

"As with the last time we had school," she began, but then paused to allow her words to uncoil slowly around the room. Her tone of voice made this simple beginning sound as if every boy in the room had committed a crime and was about to pay for it.

"As with the last time we had school," she repeated, "we will be visited by the gentlemen who oversee matters concerning the Broggin Home for Boys. With them again will be members of the Ladies' Aid and Good Works Society. I trust you will all remember to rise when they enter, and then immediately sit back down to your books. Whether you read or not is up to you, but you had better appear to be reading. Anyone who causes us any embarrassment by doing anything else will be dealt with. I am sure you all find this very clear, do you not?" Mrs. Crawler paused for exactly the amount of time needed for someone who did not value his life to respond to this question. "Well then, you may now open your books."

At that moment, along with the sound of the books being opened, came the sound of the bell ringing in the hall. Mr. Crawler leaped up so quickly he almost fell over his chair in his hurry to rush to the door. Clearly the guests arriving were very important people indeed! Moments later he was bowing them through the door. What passed for his lips, which ordinarily stretched almost from ear to ear, had somehow found a way to stretch even further in his attempt at a smile.

"As you can see," he said, piously, "the boys are hard at their reading."

Mrs. Crawler produced her own version of a smile, and sketched a curtsy that needed only the drooping pink ribbon from her night bonnet to complete the picture. Then she turned to the boys and delicately tap-tapped her hands together. "Boys, you see our guests have arrived!"

The boys instantly scrambled to their feet. And now Colley was at last able to see the people who were causing such a stir in the Broggin Home for Boys.

It was hardly to be wondered at that the gummy buns and sugar so cheerfully "pinched" by Marty had come from the larders of the three men who accompanied the ladies. For while it could not quite be said that they resembled Abigail, it was certain that they enjoyed the buns quite as much and as often as the rat. Even their somber black suits could not detract from the glow of their round pink faces or their benevolent expressions, so benevolent, in truth, that their shifty, sharp, cunning eyes were barely noticed at all.

But it was the five members of the Ladies' Aid and Good Works Society who most captured Colley's attention. All at first glance appeared to be dressed alike, so simple were the gray wool coats and capes that hung in soft folds from their slender shoulders. But what mattered most was that from under the brims of their plain hats, unadorned by a single ribbon, feather, or silk flower, they directed shy, tremulous smiles at all the boys looking back at them.

Almost at once, however, Colley had to drop dutifully back down to his seat along with the other boys, and fasten his eyes on his book. Still, he was able to hear all that was said.

"Just fine! Just fine!" said one of the men. "The boys attending to their lessons, are they?"

"Oh yes, Mr. Grimpot!" tittered a voice that Colley had difficulty in believing belonged to Mrs. Crawler.

"Their education must be seen to," said the second man sternly.

"Oh, and it is, it is, Mr. Greazle," was the soulful reply from Mr. Crawler.

"And we are certain you provide the boys with the very best, do you not?" inquired the third man in a confidential tone of voice.

"Oh, Mr. Slypenny!" replied Mrs. Crawler in what almost amounted to a moan.

"Once again you see, ladies, how much good is done by the splendid efforts and contributions of the Ladies' Aid and Good Works Society," pontificated Mr. Grimpot.

"What would we do without it?" groaned Mr. Crawler.

"And what might happen to the minds of these poor boys?" said Mrs. Crawler, sounding as if she were going to start sobbing at any moment.

After this heartrending performance, silence filled the room, presumably to let the young ladies ponder and digest it. But then a clear, light voice spoke up.

"Would it be possible for us to walk around the room, and perhaps have one or two of the boys read aloud to us from their books? I am a new member of the Ladies' Aid and Good Works Society, and this is my first visit here."

A brief, and one might say shocked silence met this request, followed by a great deal of harrumphing and clearing of throats on the part of the Messrs. Grimpot, Greazle, and Slypenny.

"Is this to be allowed, Mr. and Mrs. Crawler?" Mr. Greazle inquired silkily at last. "It seems to me that it might interfere with . . . er . . . um . . . interfere with . . ."

"The boys' studies? Why yes, indeed it would, Mr. Greazle," replied Mrs. Crawler, by now barely able to manage another titter.

"There, you see, my dear young lady," said Mr. Slypenny. "Perhaps . . ."

"Why no," interrupted the clear, light, and suddenly much firmer voice. "I don't believe I see at all. I don't see why our walking around the room and listening to a boy or two reading should take much more time than our standing here and observing. Do you *really*, Mr. Slypenny?"

"Well . . . well, perhaps not," came the reply after additional harrumphing and throat clearing. "If it might be allowed, Mr. and Mrs. Crawler?"

"If too much time is not taken with it," replied Mr. Crawler, clearly finding it difficult to keep a smile on his face.

The dainty tapping of heels on the floor denoted that the ladies had begun their journey around the room.

"I see," noted the clear, light voice, "that none of the books the boys are reading are the same. Should not some of them be studying from the same books?"

Further shock was, of course, felt while someone collected enough wits to come up with a suitable reply. It was Mrs. Crawler who was finally able to do this.

"This is their free reading time," she snapped. "They may read what they choose."

Colley wondered what the owner of the clear, light voice might think if she saw that the book he had "chosen" was an old medical book with some frightening pictures in it. But he no sooner had this thought than a delicate scent of violets wafted over him, and from the corner of his eye he saw a small white-gloved hand reach out and tap Marty on the shoulder.

"Would you care to read a little for me?" the clear, light voice asked of Marty.

Marty shifted uncomfortably on his seat, and then mumbled under his breath, "There were a rat an' a hole in the ground is where he's at. That's all there is 'bout that old rat."

Now, no one could possibly believe that in the book in front of Marty, which had to do with the mountains and rivers of the Western Hemisphere, if the title were to be believed, there appeared the words he had just "read." Remembering that Zack had had to help the boys reading the gravestones, Colley saw that Marty had needed more than just a little help. Why, he could not read at all! Would the light, clear voice remark on it?

"Thank you very much. That was very nice," was all it said. And then Colley felt a tap on his own shoulder. "Would you also read a little for me?"

Colley turned his head to catch a brief look at a sweet, smiling face before turning back to begin reading.

"Quarantine in some places is a progressive question, affected by the increasing population in the ports in which it is enforced, their influence on the surrounding land and water, the increasing number of ships at anchorage, and . . ."

Colley was stopped by another gentle tap on the shoulder. "That was very well read. Thank you so much," said the light, clear voice as it moved away.

"Is there anyone else who wishes to see more?" asked Mr. Crawler in a manner suggesting that enough was enough and nobody had better have such a wish.

"Oh, I believe that won't be necessary," said Mr. Grimpot in a voice designed to soothe ruffled waters.

"We must not be disturbing the boys at their reading any further," added Mr. Greazle.

"Nor be detaining these kind young ladies," concluded Mr. Slypenny.

As there now seemed to be nothing left for the group to do but depart, that is what they did. Then, only moments after Mr. Crawler had ushered them out, he ushered himself back in again, his wide expanse of chin quivering with fury.

"All right, you same boys, clear the table!" he snarled. "And be quick about it. The rest of you, line up!"

And so, though it was now later than usual, Colley found himself marching again to the glass works for another day of misery. But now he had been introduced to what passed for education at the Broggin Home for Boys. Small wonder that Marty had described it as a "flippin' joke."

Chapter XV

A Disturbing Encounter

Setting his lantern down on the stone step, Colley cautiously lifted the trapdoor leading from the tunnel to the graveyard. His skin felt clammy from nervousness and fear.

He had not really wanted to come, not alone anyway. He would have been happy to wait for a moonlit night and come with the other boys. But Rufus had been so proud of giving up his turn so Colley could "have a go at it," that Colley felt he could not say "no" to the offer. Now he almost wished that he had anyway.

Well, why not just *say* he had gone into the graveyard, but not really go at all? Who was there to see what he did or tell on him? The gravestones all sat silently in the ghostly light of early evening. They would say nothing. What better to keep a secret than a stone in a graveyard?

But Colley knew that the boys would want a report of his visit there. Rufus had asked him to "give a look in on" his own personal "family" gravestone, the one marked "Abner Kiley, beloved grandfather" three gravestones to the left of the trapdoor. And all the boys expected him to choose one for himself. The first thing they would want to know was the gravestone he had picked. So there was nothing for it but that he must go into the graveyard. Taking a deep gulp of air, he stepped through the trapdoor.

Almost instantly he felt there was nothing there to fear, for all around him was a curious feeling of peace and safety. And how very still and quiet it was! The noises of the city sounded distant and far away. All around him was grass, some of it ankle high, and some of it even knee high. Most of it was choked with weeds. But it was not the cold, hard, city concrete, or the chilling linoleum floor of the Broggin Home for Boys. What was under his feet now might be shaggy and unkempt, but it was green, and it was growing.

Slowly, Colley began to wander among the gravestones, seeking out the "family members" of the boys. Even without reading the stones, he knew which ones they were from the way the plots around some were carefully tended.

For Rufus, of course, there was the stone for Abner Kiley. For Zack there was Rebecca Warburton. For Toby there was Hannah Dilley. For Noah there was Josiah Bates. And for Marty there was Timothy O'Riley. And now there was a new stone to be added to their family list, the one chosen by Colley. It was marked "Samantha Trilby," taken because the last name sounded a bit like his own. He could not help wondering if the boys had chosen names that sounded like *their* own. But it was certain that as long as they were at the Broggin Home for Boys, he would never know.

His gravestone found, however, he was down on his knees at once pulling up the weeds from around it. He would never have believed such work could be so pleasant. How different it was from being at the glass works! One by one by one, the weeds went flying over his shoulders. He was so intent on his work he never even heard the gate open, much less anyone approaching him.

"Oh!" cried a startled voice. "There's someone here! I thought we were the only ones."

Colley jumped to his feet and whirled around to find a young woman standing before him. A second one, who had been bending over one of the gravestones several feet behind them, raised her head at the sound of her friend's cry, and came running over.

"Belinda, is this not the same young boy who read to you so nicely this morning?" asked the first young woman.

"Why yes, Mary, it is indeed!" exclaimed the second. "How delightful to see you again," she said, addressing Colley. "And how good it is that someone can come and take care of this almost forgotten place. Do you like to come here?"

Shocked and frightened at having been found in the graveyard, Colley could only nod his head dumbly and drop his eyes.

"Well," the young woman continued, "*I* only learned of it today, and came with my friend to see if this might not be a place where a great-great-aunt of mine might be. Her name was Rebecca Warburton, and just think, I have found her gravestone right away! It is one of the ones so beautifully tended. Was that done by you?"

Colley hesitated a moment before nodding his head again. If anyone were to get in trouble over this, it must not be Zack, but the one who got caught out there—Colley.

"Thank you then," said the young woman. Suddenly, after thinking for a moment, she added, "Have . . . have you been here at the Broggin Home for very long?"

"N-n-no," stammered Colley.

But before he could be asked further questions, a man's voice called out from the gate.

"Have you found the name yet? It is becoming dark very quickly, and we really must be going."

As all his attention had been on the two young ladies, Colley had not noticed anyone by the gate. Who was he? Standing in the shadow of the wall as he was, and in the fading light, it was impossible to tell. One quick look told Colley only that the man was very tall, and that he might be wearing a naval uniform. But it seemed to Colley that he might now have even more reason to be frightened.

"Yes, we have found the name," the young woman who had been speaking to Colley called back. "We are coming right away." Then she turned back to Colley and gave him a searching look. "Oh, I should have told you I am Miss Belinda Dorcas, and my friend is Miss Mary Reed. And what . . . what is your name?"

Once again, Colley hesitated, for he desperately wanted to say, "I am Colley Trevelyan. Please won't you help me?"

But what if Miss Dorcas were not what she appeared to be, despite her sweet face and manner? Or what if she did not think it would be proper to do anything against the rules of the Broggin Home for Boys? After all, had she not had to ask permission of Mr. Grimpot, Mr. Greazle, and Mr. Slypenny to be allowed to walk around the room that morning and ask the boys to read? And what of the man awaiting her at the gate? Might he not be a representative of those gentlemen? No, no, Colley could not dare give his real name.

"J-J-Jed Broggin," he mumbled finally.

"And is this where you are assigned to work, Jed Broggin?" Miss Dorcas asked.

"N-n-no," Colley stammered. "I . . . I go to the glass works."

"I see," said Miss Dorcas. "Well, Jed, perhaps we shall have the pleasure of hearing you read again. But we must say good-bye for now."

Waving to him, the two young women turned and made their way carefully through the grass and tall weeds. Motionless, Colley watched them, but as soon as he heard the gate close behind them, he raced for the trapdoor.

Grateful that he had closed the trapdoor, hiding any faint glow that might have come from his lantern, he flung it open, picked up the lantern, and, after closing the trapdoor behind him, flew down the stone steps and up the tunnel—only to see another lantern lighting up the face of an angry Marty flying toward him.

"Wot kept ye? Ain't ye got no idea o' time, Jed?" he said furiously. "Supper bell's gone an' if we got all the luck in the world, we might get there 'fore the line ends. Any other ways, sure an' 'tis the hole for the both o' us. Come on then!"

Wheeling around, Marty started back up the tunnel, Colley at his heels.

"I'm sorry, Marty," Colley said, gasping from trying to keep up with him. "Something kept me out there. I couldn't leave. I'll . . . I'll tell you about it as soon as we're back in our room after dinner."

"Ye'd just better do that," said Marty ungraciously. "I ain't willin' to get the hole 'less it's for a mighty fine reason!"

Chapter XVI

Terror at Midnight

"Sure an' ye couldn't help it, Jed," Marty said when they were all back in their room after dinner, gathered around his cot. "I should o' guessed it weren't yer fault. 'Twas more the fault o' all o' us for tellin' ye nobody ever comed into the graveyard 'ceptin' usselves."

"But it's the flippin' truth, Marty," Toby said. "Ain't nobody ever been in 'fore today. Jed must o' been scairt out o' his head."

"I . . . I was," said Colley. "I would have been more scared, though, if one of the ladies hadn't been that nice one that had you and me read today, Marty."

"Might be nice, Jed," said Marty. "An' might be she thinks as how we ain't treated right with our edication, but she come with them three slimy lawyers, didn't she?"

"Yes," agreed Colley. "But, Marty, I was careful and didn't answer much to her questions."

Marty's head jerked up at this. "Wot questions?"

"Oh, she just asked if I liked coming there. And she asked if I'd been at the Broggin Home for very long," replied Colley. "She . . . she wanted to know if I was the one who'd tended her aunt's gravestone because it was so nice. It was Zack's gravestone. I hope you don't mind, Zack, but I told her I was. I thought if she reported it, no use you getting in trouble along with me."

Zack's pale eyes flew open. "I'd o' never thought o' that. Whee-oo! Thank you a lot, Jed."

"Do ye think the ladies seen how you come into the grave-yard, Jed?" Marty asked.

Colley shook his head. "I expect they thought I just came in through the gate like they did. I believe they think taking care of the gravestones is a chore the Broggin boys do."

"Sure an' let's hope that," Marty said. "Then maybe they won't run 'roun' tellin' 'bout it to them lawyer friends o' theirs. Anyways, they was only two o' them, and not a lot o' others."

"Well," said Colley slowly, "There . . . there was one other per-son. It was a man standing by the gate, and he called out to them that it was getting dark and they should be going. I . . . I couldn't see him very well, so I don't know if it's anyone I've seen around here before. I was scared when I heard his voice, but I couldn't very well stare."

"No, but didn't ye get any kind o' look at all?" Marty asked anxiously.

"Not much," said Colley. "He was tall, and . . . and I think he had on a . . . a naval uniform of some sort."

Marty threw a hand to his forehead. "I think I seen him. I think I seen him more'n oncet talkin' to them lawyers. Maybe it ain't, but tall and wearin' wot ye said he was wearin' sounds close 'nough to me. Did he see ye, Jed? Don't see as how he could o'missed."

"I just don't know," replied Colley. "I just don't."

"He might o' thinked Jed were one o' the gravestones," Toby said hopefully.

"Perhaps," said Colley. "But even if he didn't see me, I'm cer-tain Miss Dorcas and Miss Reed . . . those were the two ladies . . . might most likely tell him about me. I . . . I'm truly sorry if any-thing happens about the tunnel because of me."

"Look, Jed, it weren't yer fault," Marty said quickly. "An' ain't nothin' we can do 'bout it. We just got to wait an' see wot happens.

But, Jed, I got somethin' else we got to talk 'bout. Ye never said nothin' 'bout bein' pushed when ye fell the other day at the glass works."

"But I wasn't pushed," Colley said. "I just stumbled and fell."

"Ye certain 'bout that?" Marty asked.

"I don't know," Colley replied. "It happened so quickly. I just don't remember."

· "Sure an' I'll 'member for ye," said Marty. "Ye *was* pushed. Ye was pushed by Gorp, 'cause Silas seen it happen. It's why he told ye to keep a eye out for yer back. I ain't seen Silas to talk to till 'fore dinner when ye was in the graveyard, and he told me 'bout it then. Ye was pushed, an' it weren't no flippin' love tap neither."

"But why would Gorp want to push me? Why would he want me to be hurt or . . . or even killed?" asked Colley, stunned.

"Faith an' who knows?" Marty said.

"Marty," Zack broke in, "'member wot Jed was talkin' to us 'bout . . . bein' kidnapped an' ransom an' all the rest?"

Marty nodded. "Wot ye got in mind 'bout that, Zack?"

Zack shrugged. "I ain't certain. Just seems to me as how might be somethin' added to wot Gorp done and wot Jed were sayin'. I don't really got no idea, Marty. Just somethin' not right, that's all."

"Might be," Marty said. "But I got a idea 'bout one place might say somethin'. It's that flippin' black book with red goin' down the side wot Soup seen. Somethin' might be wrote there 'bout Jed, and I aim to find out. Ain't no time to lose neither. Gorp got somethin' in mind for Jed, 'pears as how. An' look wot the Crawlers done, puttin' him in glass works, an' the scullery, an' that murderin' hole very first shot. Somethin' 'bout it don't smell right. I aim to go to the toad's hole tonight, only . . . only . . ." Marty squirmed uncomfortably. "I guess as how someone got to come with me. It . . . it ought to be Zack. You willin', Zack?"

Now, it did not take much thought to know why Marty needed someone to go with him, and why he particularly chose Zack. Marty could not read. The other boys might be able to read a little, but it was Zack, after all, who had read the names on the gravestones to them. And Marty would need someone to read whatever was written in the black book with the red spine. But why should it be Zack? Was there not someone else among them who could read just as well, and should more properly take the risk? Even as Zack was nodding his head to going, Colley spoke up.

"No, Marty, Zack isn't going with you. I . . . I am," he said. "I'm the reason anyone is going at all."

"Well, if ye really want to, Jed," Marty replied. "Then no more said 'bout it. Come midnight, we'll go."

"How will we know it's midnight?" asked Colley, who had not known the time since he came to the Broggin Home, and had wondered how, visitors aside, he would have known when to return from his graveyard visit. The other boys all seemed to have built-in timepieces.

"Ain't you never heard the church bells bongin'?" Rufus asked. "O' course you got to listen real good down here, an' mostly we're all sleepin', but them bells do bong, don't they, Marty?"

"Sure an' they do," Marty replied. "If ye'll be listenin' for 'em, ye'll hear 'em, Jed. *I* will. Don't ye have no fears 'bout that!"

Colley woke up shivering—shivering and with a murderous sore throat, the kind that was all too familiar from the past. Then, of course, Dr. Gravely had been summoned at once, leaving behind bottles of syrups and pills, and the dire warning that Colley must be kept in bed. There Colley would remain, propped up with mountains of down pillows, worried and fretted over by his mama and Lucy. Was the room too cold? Should another log be put on the fire in the fireplace? Did he want a sip of something warm to drink? Was his appetite up to a bit of roast chicken for dinner?

Instead, he was going off on a frightening mission in the dead of night at the Broggin Home for Boys. Tomorrow he would be sent off to the glass works with a crust of hard bread in his pocket.

Even so small a favor as being allowed to stay in his cot would be, as Marty would put it, a "flippin' joke." Colley drew his knees up tight to his chest, trying not to think about any of it. Perhaps the sore throat would go away. Perhaps he was only shivering because of where he had to go with Marty. Perhaps the bells had already rung and he and Marty had slept right through them and would not be going at all. He had no sooner had this thought, however, than he heard the faint ring of the church bells sounding out the hour of midnight. Immediately, Marty's bedsprings creaked and his feet thumped on the ground as he jumped from his cot.

"Ye awake, Jed?" he whispered.

"Yes," Colley whispered back.

"Ready to go?" asked Marty.

No, Colley was not ready to go, but he had determined that he would go anyway, no matter what. He would not say a word to Marty about how terrible he felt until they returned. So he hesitated only a moment before replying, "Yes, I . . . I'm ready."

"Come on, then," Marty said. "an' no shoes neither. We got to have a lantern, but I'll turn it down to just 'bout nothin'."

In moments they were creeping down the hall, their bare feet making no sound. Then up the stairs they went, through the kitchen and the dining hall, where the boys' jackets hung limp on the wall like so many small dark ghosts, then down the hall, and at last into the room where boys were brought on their first grim night at the Broggin Home for Boys.

Everything was just as Colley remembered it. Added to the stark desk and two chairs, however, was a round table with a dingy, lace-trimmed cloth over it reaching to the floor, and on top an ugly pink glass vase filled with paper flowers. This display, one might suspect, had been placed there to provide the Ladies' Aid and Good Works Society with a sample of how warm and cozy the Broggin Home could be. But the table had no drawers, so that left only the desk as the place to look for the black book. Marty found it at once in the bottom drawer. Why the drawer was left unlocked can only be guessed, and the guess would be that the Crawlers could not believe any Broggin boy who enjoyed living and breathing would dare come into that room, or rummage in the desk drawers. In any event, it was not a question Marty and Colley cared to stand around pondering. Marty simply snatched up the book and handed it to Colley, who opened it at once to where the last entry was made—that of himself.

"See here, Marty! See here!" Colley pointed to the two words next to his name.

"Wot does it say?" asked Marty.

"It's something that isn't next to anyone else's name," replied Colley. "It says 'paid us.' So it's what I thought to start with. Somebody paid Mr. and Mrs. Crawler to keep me until they could get ransom for me. I think who did it is someone who worked for our family. His name is Cark. He knows my aunt and uncle will soon return and pay it."

"Then wot's Gorp up to," Marty said. "An' how 'bout them Crawlers. Faith an' a body'd think they'd want ye in one piece so they'd keep collectin' from this feller Cark, an' maybe gettin' some o' the ransom."

"I know," Colley said. "It seems that finding this still doesn't explain everything. Anyway, I guess we've seen all that we can. Hadn't we better be getting back?"

But before Marty could reply, both boys froze. For coming down the hallway were footsteps and voices. There was no way possible to escape the room. But there sat the round table with the cloth reaching to the floor! Whether it had succeeded in warming the hearts of the Ladies' Aid and Good Works Society might never be known, but it was certain that it greatly benefited the health and lives of the boys. Dousing the lantern light, Marty grabbed Colley's hand and dove under the table, dragging Colley, but mercifully not the tablecloth, with him. Holding their breaths, hardly daring even to blink, they waited.

Chapter XVII

The Only Solution

The boys' hearts had only pounded in their chests a few times before the footsteps entered the room, accompanied by the voices of Mr. and Mrs. Crawler. They were both yawning as they lit the two oil lamps, a faint glow from which could be seen through the folds of the tablecloth.

"It does seem to me, Obadiah," said Mrs. Crawler, "that we could arrange a better time of day to bring them in. My beauty sleep is sadly interrupted by these late night arrivals."

"My dear Quintilla," returned Mr. Crawler, "allow me to say that though your sleep may be interrupted, your beauty remains as always. You are, if I may say so, lovelier than ever. But as you know, I too have always wished that deliveries could be made during daylight hours. I must say, though, that we make more of an impression on them at this hour."

"We do indeed," said Mrs. Crawler, her tone of voice suggesting that a thin, evil smile was creeping across her face. "But, of course, if we have played our cards right, we might not be having to concern ourselves with admissions much longer."

"As to that, Quintilla, my pet," said Mr. Crawler, "since the . . . um . . . event has not yet occurred, and may take a little longer than anticipated, we may yet . . . er . . . negotiate further to our advantage. If you understand my meaning."

"And what of Gorp?" snapped Mr. Crawler's beloved.

"Hmmm," hummed Mr. Crawler. "Yes, well, I'm sure we can work things out there. But now I believe our delivery is here. Come, come, Soup, bring them in."

Thud, shhhh. Thud, shhhh. Soup was heard entering the room, accompanied by other shuffling footsteps. Then a strange voice spoke.

"Here he is. Brung as promised."

There followed a few moments of silence, presumably as what was "brung" was being examined. As nothing was said about removing any covers, it was also to be presumed that the delivery did not arrive in the same manner as Colley.

"Your opinion, Mrs. Crawler?" asked Mr. Crawler.

Mrs. Crawler sniffed. Then sniffed again. "He'll do, Mr. Crawler. You can pay up."

"Here then," said Mr. Crawler. "Terms agreed upon. And now the transaction is concluded, Mr. . . . um . . . Mr. Smith, there's no more reason for you to remain. Soup, see him out."

"No need to wait," said Mrs. Crawler. "You might as well get on with it."

"Quite right! Quite right!" agreed Mr. Crawler. And then began the speech so horribly familiar to Colley.

"You've been brought to the Broggin Home for Boys where you will be schooled, fed, and clothed, and for all of which blessings you will be expected to work."

The scene rolled on as Colley's whole nightmare was reenacted for him. It ended only when Soup and the newest Broggin "delivery," now to be known as Moses, went thumping out the door. The lamps were turned off, and the Crawlers were then heard leaving. It was not until a door was heard to close on their footsteps, that Marty and Colley finally crawled out from behind the tablecloth.

With Colley clutching the back of Marty's nightshirt, they somehow made their way back to their room in total darkness, for who would be so foolhardy as to carry a lighted lantern now? But when they arrived at the room, they were greeted by a tiny flicker of lantern light coming from the far end. And seated on Marty's cot, awaiting his and Colley's arrival with wide, excited eyes, were Noah, Toby, Rufus, and Zack!

"You look like you both seen ghosts," was Toby's greeting. "Wot did you find out 'bout Jed?"

"Sure an' we found out *somethin'*," Marty said. "But wot we found on top o' that was usselves in the very room with them Crawlers, come to give greetin's to a new wictim!"

The jaws of the whole audience of four dropped.

"Wot did they say to you?" Noah asked.

"How many nights o' the hole they givin' you?" asked Toby.

Zack shook his head in disbelief. "Yer lifes ain't worth as much as that flippin' penny now."

"But . . . but they never even saw us!" Colley burst out.

"Wot do you mean, never seen you?" Rufus said. "Where was you while they was there?"

"Faith an' ain't they just gone an' put a table there now?" replied Marty. "An' they got a cloth on top goin' all the way down so anyone wot has a need can go hidin' under it. Atop the table they even got flowers."

"Flowers!" exclaimed Toby. "Real live flowers?"

"Hmmmmph!" snorted Marty. "Real live *paper* flowers, made by usselves, I don't got a doubt."

"But so far you ain't telled us 'bout Jed. Wot was it you found out 'fore you went hidin' under them paper flowers?"

"Jed, ye tell 'em," Marty said. "Tell 'em wot we found in that black book."

"Well, it's that Mr. and Mrs. Crawler paid money for all the other boys," Colley said. "But it looks as if they were *given* money for me. Perhaps it's just what I thought, that someone is paying them to keep me until they get ransom for me. Marty thinks the Crawlers might get some of that as well."

"But then why ain't ye bein' treated better if yerself's worth all that flippin' money?" Marty said. "Glass works ain't my idea o' bein' treated like a royal highness. An' wot was them Crawlers talkin' 'bout when they was mentionin' Gorp, wot was tryin' to push ye into kingdom come, for all we know. Jed, I don't mean to scare you none, but sure an' I got a creepy feelin' 'bout it all. Just wish we could o' learned more from them two lovebirds 'fore their wictim come into the room."

"Wasn't the two o' you scairt out o' yer wits hidin' under that table?" Noah asked, shuddering.

"Faith an' does a fly got wings?" said Marty, grinning. "Them paper flowers must o' been dancin' over our heads from the shakin' goin' on under them."

"Well, Jed's still shakin'," Zack said. "More like shiverin'. You don't look too good, Jed. You still scairt?"

"Not . . . not exactly," mumbled Colley. "I . . . I didn't want to tell you before we went, Marty, but I . . . I don't believe I'm feeling very well."

All traces of the grin on Marty's face instantly vanished. "Sure an' why didn't ye say so 'fore this? Ye shouldn't o' gone. Goin' might o' made ye worse. I thought as how I felt ye shiverin' under the table, but I was shiverin' inside from bein' scairt, an' I just thought ye was shiverin' outside from bein' just as scairt. Zack, how 'bout ye takin' Jed's tempater."

Zack instantly came up to Colley and laid a small, wiry hand on his forehead as the boys all watched anxiously. Zack's lips moved silently as he counted off what he considered to be enough seconds.

"Wot do ye think, Zack?" Marty asked.

"Hotter'n a boiled potato," Zack diagnosed solemnly. "He's got somethin' all right. Wot else you got asides the shiverin', Jed?"

"My . . . my throat hurts a lot," said Colley, hesitating. He did not want to appear a baby making too many complaints.

"Throat hurts, eh?" said Zack, narrowing his eyes at hearing this interesting additional symptom. "Chest not feelin' too good neither? Wot I mean is, is it badder'n wot you been feelin' just from the glass works?"

"I think so," replied Colley. "I . . . I mean, yes it is."

"Wot do ye think, Zack?" Marty asked anxiously. "It ain't the same as wot the other Jed were ailin' from, do ye think?"

Zack rubbed his chin thoughtfully, looking grave. "Sorry, Marty, but it's exact the same, I'm afeered."

Marty groaned. "No! Can't be! Wot are we goin' to do? I ain't goin' to lose me a Jed again. I just ain't! But wot can we do if them Crawlers make him go to work. He'll get kilt by the glass works, an' seems like nothin' we can do 'bout it."

"Marty," Noah spoke up. "Don't you 'member wot we was all sayin' oncet how we should o' hid Jed in the tunnel so's he could o' never got sent to the glass works when he got sick?"

"Noah's right, Marty!" Rufus said excitedly. "That's just wot we said."

But Marty shook his head. "Sure an' we did say it, but don't ye 'member just as well that we was all askin' wot Jed would o' done oncet he weren't sick no more? If he runned off, he would o' just got picked up and sent to worse. Or wot if he would o' come runnin' back and turned hisself in? Anyone here got a picter of a body comin' to the front door o' the Broggin Home for Boys and sayin', 'Halloo, Crawlers, I made a mistake 'bout runnin' off, an' I come back!'? He would o' ended up kilt for certain as a sample for the rest o' us."

"Marty, he were kilt anyways," Zack said gently. "Hid in the tunnel, he'd o' had a bit o' a chance. Wot he got were none."

Marty sat for a few moments biting his lip and staring down at his cot. "Faith an' I got no idea why I'm arguin' 'bout it. Yer all right. 'Twould be nice if them Crawlers might o' growed hearts an' not sent ailin' boys off to the glass works, but hearts ain't in the picter. An' Jed ain't just ailin' neither. Somethin's goin' on 'bout him wot's smellin' fishy. Ailin' or not, it 'pears as how maybe it just ain't safe for him to stay. One chance is better'n no chance, an' the tunnel's the onliest one we got. If . . . if . . . I'm meanin' *when* he gets well, we'll decide wot's best to do then."

"Well, nobody's asked me what *I* think," Colley blurted. "And it's no use your talking about me staying in the tunnel, because I won't!"

"Sure an' why not?" Marty asked, looking at him with disbelief, seeming to forget that a few moments earlier he himself had had to be persuaded of the idea.

"Because if I do," replied Colley, "they'll come looking for me. Don't think they won't be looking *everywhere*, and more than likely will find the tunnel. They'll find *me* in it, and you won't have the tunnel anymore. Did anyone think about that?"

It was clear from the looks on the boys' faces that no one had. For a few moments there was a stunned silence. Then at last Marty grinned.

"Sure an' don't meself know just where ol' Boiler keeps the key hangin' to the back door leadin' to the alley? I heerd Soup say as how Boiler don't 'member to lock the door like he ought lots o' times 'cause o' how he comes rollin' in nights. I'll see the door ain't locked tonight, an' doors is the first place they'll go lookin'. If a door ain't locked, wot do ye suppose they'll be thinkin'? Ye got more questions 'bout that, Jed?"

Colley shook his head as smiles spread across all faces present.

"But wot 'bout food, an' drink, an' . . . an' facilities?" Noah asked. "Jed can't live down there with none o' them, an' ailin' besides."

"Well," Marty said thoughtfully, "there's gummy buns. Jed'll get all o' them, 'ceptin' maybe a bit for Abigail. That rat's gettin' too fat, so he don't need much for a while. We got to see later wot else we can find."

"We got that big bottle down there for carryin' water," Toby said eagerly. "An' there's lots o' cups for Jed to drink out o'."

"But wot 'bout facilities?" Rufus asked. "Ain't no way to pervide *them*."

"How 'bout the graveyard?" Zack said.

"Don't seem right," Marty replied. "But sure an' ye'll have to use that, Jed."

But Toby then grabbed his forehead. "Wot's Jed goin' to do for a bed? Can't take his cot nor his blanket from here. No one wot runs off takes their bed with 'em wot I ever knowed 'bout."

"Well, I'm leavin' now so's I can take care o' the door," Marty said. "When I'm comin' back, I'll stop and help meself to a blanket'r two from Soup's cupboard. Jed, ye best get into yer clothes an' leave yer nightshirt behind. Tobe's right 'bout nobody runnin' off takin' their bed with 'em, an' likewise nobody runs off wearin' their nightshirt neither. I'll be back quicker'n a wink."

It seemed that Colley hardly had time to climb into his shirt and trousers before Marty was back with blankets, and Toby had brought up the bottle from the tunnel and filled it with water from the hall sink. Then the boys all climbed into the tunnel with Colley. In no time, they had made up a bed for him on the floor and seen to it that he was safely lying down in it. Then beside him they set the bottle of water, one of the chipped cups, and the half gummy bun still remaining in the cupboard. This all taken care of, Zack leaned over, once again laid a wiry hand on Colley's forehead, and directed a gloomy glance at Marty.

"Now ye take care, Jed," Marty said, attempting a smile. "One o' us'll be down in the mornin' to check on ye. An' don't ye worry 'bout nothin'."

"You'll be all right," Noah said.

"Never fear," said Rufus.

"We'll be seein' you," added Toby.

"Just see you get yer rest," concluded Zack with a warning frown.

"'Night, Jed!" Marty said.

"'Night!"

"'Night!"

"'Night!"

"'Night!"

Each boy called out over his shoulder as he climbed the ladder. And then Colley was alone in the tunnel, left staring at the tiny, flickering light of the lantern on the floor near where he lay.

How kind the boys—no, not the boys, his *friends*—had been to him, and how grateful he was that he did not have to return to the glass works in the morning. But was it enough? Would Marty lose another Jed? Colley had always known himself to be "frail." Could he get well without Dr. Gravely and his bottles of potions and pills, without a dainty diet, piles of down pillows under his head, and anxious parents and servants hovering over him? Could he survive on a hard floor in a dank tunnel with half a gummy bun, a cup of water, and a fluttering lantern beside him, his only companion a large rat in a box somewhere off in the darkness?

Chapter XVIII

A Dread Voice Returned

The days that followed his first night in the tunnel all became a blur in Colley's mind. He never knew if it were night or day, or how many days passed. Was it just one? Or two? Or three? Or more? The time seemed to melt together with nothing to separate one minute, one hour, one day, from the other.

And who was the boy, or boys, kneeling down beside him to lift his burning, aching head to make him take sips of water, or eat tiny bits of gummy bun, feed him as if he were a baby, or hold him up while he went to visit the graveyard "facility"? Sometimes he recognized the boys' faces. Sometimes he did not. Once he thought it was Lucy beside him.

But then one unforgettable night, Colley felt the familiar cool, small, wiry hand on his forehead, and heard a voice say, "Ain't quite so hot, Marty."

"Ye sure, Zack?" came the quick reply. "Ye ain't made no mistake?"

"I know wot hot feels like," said Zack indignantly. "An' I say he ain't so hot."

"That means he's gettin' better, don't it?" Marty asked eagerly.

"Means it to me," said the medical expert calmly.

And it was true. Colley was indeed getting better. It seemed a miracle, but there was no denying it.

"Should I call the others down?" Marty asked. "Wot do ye think, Zack?"

Zack returned his hand to Colley's forehead. "Gettin' better like I said, but the others can see him in the mornin'. Right now wot Jed needs is his sleep."

Jed! Who was that, Colley wondered groggily. He came close to telling them that there was some mistake being made, but remembered in time. Yes, he *was* Jed, and these were Marty and Zack. Somewhere up above were Noah and Rufus and Toby. All five of them were his friends. They had saved his life, and all they had had by way of medicines were gummy buns and water. It was the last thought Colley had before, for the first time in days, he fell into a deep and peaceful sleep.

Colley, of course, did not recover in an instant. He remained weak for a while and still needed the care of the boys. But each day he grew stronger, and the beaming faces gathered around him were grand medicine indeed!

Gummy buns as daily fare did not have quite the attraction they once had, but the boys brought down an occasional cup of stew stolen from the kitchen. Colley tried not to think of where some of the ingredients might have come from as he ate it. Three times too, Marty proudly presented him with an apple taken from a sack brought into their offices by "them lawyers." Something else, however, taken from the same source, did not please Colley at all.

Marty had discovered that Mr. Greazle fancied himself as having delicate health, so he had a cabinet full of various remedies to improve his condition. One remedy in a bottle with a large fish pictured on the label had clearly not pleased Mr. Greazle's palate, for it was pushed, largely untouched, to the back of the cabinet packed with other tins and bottles. This was cod liver oil. Zack read the words to Colley from the label. He was forced, under threat of terrible consequences if he refused, to choke down large gulps of the oil. He also learned that while he was very ill, some gummy bun bits fed to him had been dipped in it. "It were probable wot cured you," said Zack. Colley, familiar with the terrible tasting cod liver oil from his past life, disagreed, for he did not believe it had ever cured him of anything before. No, it was the gummy buns that had done it, plus the good nursing care he had received, and so he would have argued with Dr. Gravely, who would no doubt have agreed with Zack.

This argument, however—held between Colley, Zack, and Marty—only went to prove that Colley was truly well. Well enough, indeed, to hear from Marty the sad news that when it had been discovered that the back door was unlocked, it was Soup who was blamed for not having checked it. For the very first time, he had been sentenced to the hole! The boys had, of course, visited him that night, and could tell that he had been crying. Sadly, Colley knew that there was probably no way he could ever make it up to that poor young man.

Once Colley was entirely recovered, it could not be denied that plans must be made for what was to happen to him. It could not be put off much longer. After all, he could not, like Abigail, be expected to live in the tunnel forever. Even though the boys brought him scraps of newspaper pages found blowing about in the streets or an occasional crumpled magazine page, for they knew, as Marty put it, that "Jed were a good reader," it was hardly enough to fill the long, deadly hours. And even though it was now into spring and the weather was warm enough that Colley could, with great care, spend more time in the graveyard, it was felt that a decision must be made as to what was to become of him.

At last they decided that the following night when they met in the tunnel, they would do nothing but talk about this, and perhaps someone would come up with an idea as to what was to be done, though in truth nobody's hopes were very high on this score. For what possibilities were there beyond those they had talked over again and again and found to be hopeless? Still, the attempt must be made.

That afternoon Colley went out in the graveyard, keeping his eyes and ears sharpened for the sight or sound of someone coming through the gate. He wandered about as he always did, then ended up lying on his back in the grass and weeds, staring up at the patch of sky overhead. Two birds came flying in over the wall, hopping from gravestone to gravestone before flying back out again, and Colley wondered if they might not be the sparrows Marty talked about. It was all so warm and pleasant that he finally dozed off, waking later with a start to see that the patch of sky was darkening. The boys would soon be returning from work, and he knew that one at least would be coming down into the tunnel to visit with him, perhaps bringing him a fresh gummy bun from Marty or, it might be hoped, another apple. Colley decided he had better be there to await their arrival so they would not have to come looking for him.

As he stepped down through the trapdoor, however, and leaned over to pick up his lantern, he heard curious loud crashing, banging sounds echoing down the tunnel, and with them the sound of voices that made his blood freeze. For they were the voices of Mr. and Mrs. Crawler! Somehow or other they had discovered the tunnel. How? What were they now doing? And what were they saying? Their words were nothing but hollow echoes by the time they reached Colley, so it was impossible to make them out. Still, there was no mistaking the source, and Colley had no intention of getting closer to find out what was being said, or waiting to see if they came closer to him.

Swiftly, he turned off the low flame in his lantern, picked it up and climbed out the trapdoor, closing it softly behind him. Then he ran to the far corner of the graveyard where several ragged bushes grew and the weeds were tallest. There he ducked down behind one of the larger gravestones, crouched and waited.

He did not have to wait long, for just as he expected, he heard the trapdoor being flung open, and the Crawlers came climbing noisily into the graveyard.

"So here's where those scoundrels must come!" shouted Mr. Crawler in a rage.

"Oh, and think of such villains in this sacred place!" said Mrs. Crawler prayerfully.

"Wickedness, indeed, Quintilla," said Mr. Crawler.

"And such ingratitude, Obadiah, for all we have done for them," said Mrs. Crawler. "We rescue them from the streets, feed them well, clothe them, school them, and keep their idle hands busy with honest labor. And look how we are dealt with!"

"But they will pay for this! They will pay mightily!" returned Mr. Crawler furiously.

"I pray that they will," said Mrs. Crawler. "And do you realize, too, Obadiah, that these young knaves could have escaped any time through that gate, for I see no lock on it. We must have done our work well in impressing on them the folly of such a rash venture. You don't suppose, however, that this is how Jed escaped?"

"Very likely, very likely," replied Mr. Crawler.

"And, of course, Soup punished for it," said Mrs. Crawler.

"He needed it," said Mr. Crawler. "He's been getting much too comfortable here. Leaving a door unlocked! He'll not do that again, I'll venture. But we must find Jed. That we must do."

"And what if we don't, Obadiah?" inquired Mrs. Crawler.

"Oh, we will, we will. Never fear," said Mr. Crawler. "By now we might even find him dead in a ditch."

"Dead? And how are we to explain that?" inquired Mrs. Crawler.

"*Explain?*" exploded Mr. Crawler. "Why, we'll take *credit* for it, my pet. Yes, we'll take credit for it. But of one thing you may be certain—no boy from the Broggin Home will ever escape through this place again. We'll nail their escape door so tight gunpowder can't blast it open, not to mention keeping a closer watch on those young villains and not leave it all to Soup. How fortunate I thought to look under their beds, or this would never have been discovered."

"Shall we nail this entry into the graveyard as well?" asked Mrs. Crawler.

"Might as well," said Mr. Crawler. "I'll come around and take care of it. But we must take care of the other right away before the boys return from work. Then we'll bide our time."

"Oh, how I would love to see the looks on their wily little faces when they find that slab of wood nailed shut," said Mrs. Crawler.

"I too," said Mr. Crawler. "But we'll let them discover it for themselves. By the looks of the place, they appear to use it often, so we won't have to wait long. Let them make the discovery and then ponder their fate for a while."

"Oh, Obadiah, I can't wait!" said Mrs. Crawler.

"Nor I, my beloved, nor I!" replied Mr. Crawler.

Poor Marty! Poor Zack! Poor Noah! Poor Rufus! Poor Toby! What was to become of them? What was in store for them? And what could Colley do about it? Nothing! It was always that now—nothing!

Taken up with dread over what was to happen to his friends, for a few minutes Colley did not give a thought to what was to happen to *him*. Then, with a shock, it came to him what a desperate situation he himself was in.

It was certain there would now be no meeting that night to discuss his future. There would be no meeting in that cozy den again—ever! And would his friends not wonder what would happen, what in truth *had* happened to him just as he would wonder about them? Think what good care they had taken of him only to have it come to this! And what was *this* to be? It was that he must run away, must risk the dangers of the streets, must more than anything risk being brought right back to the Broggin Home for Boys and whatever fate awaited him there. And might that fate not include his very life being ended, if one were to read anything into those chilling words spoken by Mr. and Mrs. Crawler?

The trapdoor to the tunnel was to be nailed shut, so there was no possibility of Colley living there for so much as one day longer. And how long could he live in the graveyard without food or water? No, there was no choice but to run away from it. He would have to leave that very night, hoping to run fast enough and far enough to be out of reach of the long arms of Mr. and Mrs. Crawler. It seemed hopeless, but he would have to try.

His best plan, he decided, would be to try to hide by day and travel by night, at least until he felt he was far enough away to be safe. Water he could find, drinking from ditches if he must. After all, he was far less particular than he had been before being at the Broggin Home. As for food, he would have to consider those sources of materials that went into a Broggin stew, the sweepings and refuse from the backs of stores and eating establishments. Or he might just have to pinch something, as Marty would put it. But his purpose was somehow to find his way back to his home, miles away though it was. Lucy would take him in if nothing else. And perhaps his Uncle Jasper and Aunt Serena might have returned by now. No matter what, they could not help but be relieved to have him walk through the door alive. He would then try to get word to his friends that he was safe. And perhaps some day he could try to rescue *them* from the Broggin Home, although at that moment it seemed it would surely be impossible.

But as he crouched in the graveyard awaiting nightfall, he suddenly remembered something. Abigail! How could he go off and leave the boys' pet in a box in the tunnel to die? No, he could not let that happen to Abigail. Of course, he could not carry the box with him, but he could release Abigail into the graveyard. There he would have a chance to survive. Colley dreaded the thought of going back into the tunnel now, but he must do so. And at once.

Grateful that Marty had insisted he must always keep a box of matches in his pocket, Colley was now able to make his way down the tunnel with a lantern, wondering how he would have fared if he had to find his way to Abigail in total darkness. But when he reached the boys' den, before going to pick up Abigail's box, he raised the lantern for one last look, and then gave a cry of horror at what he saw before him.

The boxes lay strewn across the floor, most of them smashed. The cupboard made of boxes was knocked over, and pieces of cups and plates lay everywhere. As for the pictures, they were all ripped off the walls, mostly torn to bits. Tears flew to Colley's eyes when he saw what was once a part of the picture of a ship, so proudly pointed out by Noah, and the picture of a dog, claimed by Zack. For no reason that he could think of, Colley picked up both pieces and stuffed them in his pocket. Then he found something else that he hid under his shirt—two gummy buns that must have rolled from the cupboard when it came tumbling down and were some-how missed by Mr. and Mrs. Crawler. The buns would keep him going for two days if he was careful.

Colley knew he could spend no more time in the tunnel. He must get Abigail and leave. But then he realized that with all his attention given to the terrible scene of destruction, he had not even looked to see if Abigail's box was in its usual place. What if the Crawlers had smashed that box as well and Abigail was now lost in the tunnel? But to his great joy, the box was just where it always had been, and Abigail in it.

It was a struggle for Colley to carry the heavy box down the tunnel and up the stairs to the graveyard, his lantern dangling from one crooked finger. But at last he managed it, and stumbled across the graveyard, setting the box down behind the same gravestone where he had hidden from the Crawlers.

It was dark enough now that Colley knew he could leave. Lifting the top, he tipped the box on its side so Abigail could crawl out. Then, hoping no one had had the chance to note the light, he quickly put out the lantern. It would, of course, have to be left behind.

"Well, good-bye, Abigail," he whispered. "I . . . I hope you'll be all right."

But he had no sooner started off through the gravestones, than he turned back and reached into his shirt. Pulling out a gummy bun, he laid it outside the box.

"There," he said. "One for you, and one for me."

Then once again he started for the gate. Having managed to reach it safely without running into any gravestones along the way, he opened it cautiously and crept out. He had taken no more than five steps, however, when a man's hand clamped over his mouth, and a voice hissed in his ear.

"If you value your life, don't struggle or make a sound!"

Colley recognized the voice, for it belonged to someone he knew. It was the voice of—Cark!

Chapter XIX

A Stranger Revealed

Colley fully expected that he would be led right down the street and ushered back into the Broggin Home for Boys. Instead, Cark, with a steely grip on Colley's arm, summoned a cab.

"Now don't you do anything foolish like trying to escape out that other door, Master Colley," Cark said as he sent Colley up into the cab, following close behind. "It won't do you any good because I'll be right after you. You just sit there quietly, and no harm will come to you."

The cab started up with a jolt, and after that there was no sound to be heard but the clop-clopping of the horses' hooves. Cark directed an occasional sidelong glance at Colley, but beyond that he sat staring silently ahead as the cab rolled on and on, down one gaslit street and up another. Where were they going? And who would be there when they finally arrived? Could it possibly be to someplace worse than the Broggin Home for Boys, and to someone worse than Mr. and Mrs. Crawler? Was he being taken to be a breaker boy in the coal mines, something so dreaded by his friends? And if that were the case, what could he do about it, being back in Cark's clutches as he was? Nothing! Again and again and again—nothing! *Clop! Clop! Clop!*

Then, at long last, the cab pulled to a stop. They were still in the city and had stopped before a narrow brick house set in a row of other equally narrow houses. Iron railings led up brick steps to a polished oak door framed with brass lamps lit for the night. This could not be a coal mine, Colley thought. Perhaps that horror would come later.

His hand tightly around Colley's arm again, Cark led him from the cab and up the brick steps. Cark pressed a button, which produced a loud ring just inside the door. It had the distinct sound of a ship's bell. In a moment the door was flung open to reveal a tall, broad-shouldered young man in navy blue trousers and a navy sweater with a collar that went high about his neck. It was difficult to tell, since Colley's view of the man standing at the gate of the graveyard when he had been found by the two ladies had been slight, but he felt certain that this was the very same man!

And was he not, therefore, the same man Marty believed he had seen talking on several occasions to "them lawyers"? And were those three gentlemen, Messrs. Grimpot, Greazle, and Slypenny, not the very ones who were deep in the pockets of all affairs connected with the Broggin Home for Boys? Why had Colley been brought to this man? Was he, after all, to be taken right back and thrust into the murdering hands of Mr. and Mrs. Crawler?

"I found him, Captain," Cark said. "I have to say after so many days, I was ready to give up on it. A few more minutes and I would have left the place, when there he appeared, scuttling out of the graveyard."

The man stared at Colley with piercing eyes. "You're certain about this?" he asked. "You know I have to rely on you completely, Simon."

"I never saw him that many times, Captain, but I have a sharp eye, and I'm certain," Cark said. "You can count on it."

"Well, good work then," the man said. "But can you be just as certain you weren't seen?"

"The street outside the graveyard was all but empty," Cark replied.

"And the street outside here?" the man asked.

"Only one empty cab going the other direction," Cark said. "I sent my cab off. When I leave, I'll go by the back and get another one when I need it."

"Good!" the man said. "That would be safest. Now, if you'll be kind enough to wait for me in my study, I'll take the boy upstairs. I'm going to be writing some short letters that will need to be delivered tonight. I'd like you to take them for me, if you would. Come along with me, Colley!"

But Colley stood motionless as if nailed to the spot where he stood. Then he gave a start. *He* was Colley! He had almost forgotten that. But though Cark had known his name, how did this man? Who was he?

"Come on! It's all right. You're only going to your room," the man said, standing aside as Colley finally began to climb the stairs. The man followed him up.

When they reached the top, he led Colley into a small room containing only a narrow bed, a chest, and a chair, but it was very neat and sparkling clean.

"I'll leave you now," the man said. "My housekeeper, Mrs. Trimble, will be right up to show you where to wash, and to bring you your supper. Try not to be frightened. I believe everything will turn out all right."

He turned and started out the door. Then he hesitated and turned back again. "Look, you'll be learning a great deal tomorrow. I'm sorry I'm so preoccupied, but I have much on my mind. Still, I think there is something you really should know now, and that is who I am. Well, Colley, I'm Jeremy Trevelyan—your *cousin* Jeremy."

Chapter XX

A Startling Scene

C olley slept late the following morning, awakened by Mrs. Trimble bringing him a tray with two hot muffins and butter, a dish of sliced apples, and a cup of milk. He looked at the small clock on the wall and saw that it was already ten o'clock, suddenly realizing that it was the first time in days—or perhaps weeks—that he had known the time of day. But he was told by Mrs. Trimble that he must hurry through his breakfast, remove the oversized garment lent him as a nightshirt, and climb into his own clothes quickly, for the captain was to leave soon, and Colley was to go with him.

But where were they to go? Cark was in the hallway when Colley came down the stairs, and it appeared that he was to accompany them. But why? Captain Trevelyan—Jeremy—now wearing his naval uniform, said nothing about it as they left the house and climbed into the cab that had been summoned. In truth, he said very little at all, and both he and Cark were remarkably silent.

But as they were seating themselves in the cab, Jeremy said, "See here, Colley, I'm sorry again not to be more conversational, but as I said last night, I do have much to think about. I want to say to you, however, that you must try not to be frightened by what you might be about to see and hear. Believe me when I say it will be far more disturbing to me than to you. Try to remember that, will you?"

Puzzled by this curious warning, Colley could think of nothing to say, so he simply nodded. After that, the inside of the cab fell silent. And once again, the cab went up one street and down another, Colley recognizing none of them. But all at once he realized that the buildings he saw outside the window had begun to look somewhat familiar. And then more and more familiar, until at last they came to a building so familiar Colley almost stopped breathing at the sight of it. Two carriages were already pulled up in front of its doorway, and the cab he was in joined them. The building, announced a shabby sign on its wall, was—the Broggin Home for Boys!

Colley felt that his knees would give out from under him as they climbed from the cab. He began to tremble as they stood before the door, and Cark reached out to ring the doorbell. Then Colley felt the strong hand of his Cousin Jeremy on his shoulder, squeezing it.

"I know! I understand!" Jeremy said softly. "But be brave. It will all be over soon."

Be brave! Yes, Colley would have to try, for what else was there to do? But, oh, could Jeremy possibly know or even imagine what the Broggin Home for Boys was all about? Colley shuddered as heavy footsteps approached the door, and it was flung open to reveal—Mr. Crawler!

"Good morning!" said the young captain pleasantly. "I am Captain Trevelyan, and this is Mr. Cark. I believe some people are here who are expecting me. Would you be kind enough to escort us to them?"

"Oh, to be sure, to be sure," replied Mr. Crawler as he grandly bowed in the new arrivals. But then his eyes fell on Colley, who had been standing partly hidden by his tall cousin. Mr. Crawler's face immediately began the battle of trying to look overjoyed at the return of this boy while masking his true feelings of red-hot fury. Joy, of necessity, won out, but undoubtedly fooled no one present.

"And what have we here?" Mr. Crawler said with a ghastly grin. "Where did you find this young scamp? He's been missing for days, you know. Had us worried to death. But he appears to be back. Well, we'll deal with him now. Come along, Jed."

"Not quite so fast," said the captain, putting a hand out to hold Colley back. "We'll keep . . . *Jed* with us for a while, if you don't mind. Now, if you'll just lead the way."

"Oh, certainly, certainly," said Mr. Crawler, his chin quivering with suppressed rage. Giving Colley a baleful look, he wheeled abruptly around and started down the hallway.

Just before they entered the dining hall, Jeremy reached out and once more squeezed Colley's shoulder. It was well that Colley had received that squeeze, for what a startling scene greeted them when they passed through the doors!

At the long table were seated all the Broggin boys, books open before them as they were once again being put on display. Soup stood cowering in a far corner of the room. A few feet from the head of the table stood Mrs. Crawler, attempting to keep a thin smile from vanishing from her face. To one side of her stood the Messrs. Grimpot, Greazle, and Slypenny, looking uncertain as to whether the occasion called upon them to be cheerful or solemn or both. Beside them stood Miss Belinda Dorcas, who did not seem to feel the need to pretend anything as she looked sympathetically at the boys. At her side was a handsome, gray-haired man in a sea captain's uniform.

Completing this cast of characters was a man wearing what was clearly an extraordinarily expensive suit and at least three heavy gold chains stretched across his vest. Accompanying him was a woman equally elegantly and expensively dressed, her neck draped in heavy strands of what could only have been the most valuable of real pearls. These last two were Jeremy's father and step-mother, Colley's uncle and aunt—Jasper and Serena Trevelyan!

All eyes were riveted on the tall young captain as he strode through the doorway. As soon as Mr. Trevelyan's eyes fell on his son, he held out his arms.

"Jeremy, Jeremy, at long last we see you again!"

"Yes, Father," Jeremy said, going up to him. But he hardly returned his father's embrace with the same feeling, for his own was stiff and uncomfortable. Then he turned to his stepmother, embracing her in the same stiff manner. "Serena, how are you?"

"But, my dear boy," said Mr. Trevelyan. "Why did you insist to Mr. Grimpot that we must meet here, of all strange places?"

"Because of your connection with it, Father," said Jeremy simply. "And to assure that no one was given the opportunity to do away with proofs needed to bring the right people to justice."

"I'm afraid, Jeremy, the sea has taught you to talk in riddles," said Mr. Trevelyan, forcing a smile. "But may I ask what connection I could possibly have with the Broggin Home for Boys?"

"Oh, come now, Father," Jeremy replied. "Let's not play games, the kind you used on me as a boy. But perhaps you haven't noticed whom I have brought with me." He stepped aside and put an arm around Colley, who had been standing all but hidden behind him.

The eyes of the boys around the table, and most especially those of Marty, Zack, Noah, Rufus, and Toby, flew open so wide it almost seemed their eyeballs would pop right out.

Mr. Crawler had, of course, already had the opportunity of show-ing how he felt about Colley's appearance. As for Mrs. Crawler, it can only be said that if looks could be bottled, hers would certain-ly have been in one with a label picturing a skull and crossbones. It was to the credit of his cousin's arm around his shoulders that Colley did not perish on the spot.

Miss Dorcas smiled at Colley, as did the sea captain by her side.

But the faces of Messrs. Grimpot, Greazle, and Slypenny, as well as the faces of Mr. and Mrs. Trevelyan, turned ashen.

"C-C-Colley!" stammered Mr. Trevelyan. "My . . . my dear boy! Where have you been all this time? We . . . we thought you were no more. Come here to us, Nephew!"

Nephew! At the sound of the word, and as Colley walked slowly over to have his head patted gingerly by his aunt and uncle before returning to stand by Jeremy, Mr. and Mrs. Crawler's faces rapidly transformed from looks of fury, to shock, to horror, to craven fear. Mr. Crawler's enormous chin began to quiver like a bowl of pale jelly.

"Y-y-your nephew?" said Mr. Crawler. "Oh, Mr. Grimpot! Oh, Mr. Greazle! Oh, Mr. Slypenny! You might have told us. We would never have agreed to . . . that is to say, we never would have . . ." He stopped in a state of panic and confusion.

"Never would have what, Mr. Crawler?" inquired young Captain Trevelyan. "Never would have agreed with Mr. Gorp and his associates to help speed a young boy to kingdom come for a large monetary reward? I must inform you, Mr. and Mrs. Crawler, that it makes little difference that you did not know who your young victim really was. Murder is still murder!"

"Murder!" exclaimed Mr. Trevelyan. "Was Colley brought here to be murdered? What are you talking about, Jeremy?"

"Oh, Father, as if you didn't know," said Jeremy, shaking his head sadly. "Do you mean to say you didn't agree to having him kidnapped and brought here, knowing that he could hardly survive this grim place for very long? That he survived to be standing here today certainly points to more spunk and spirit than he was ever credited with."

"How dare you, Jeremy!" said Mr. Trevelyan, struggling to control the anger in his voice. "The whole idea is preposterous! And even if not, how, I ask you, could I have been a party to it? Your stepmother and I have been abroad for all these many weeks, and only just returned. I received word by cable from Grimpot that Colley had apparently threatened to run off, had then done so and had never been found. So he was presumed dead."

"Yes, yes, quite true," Mr. Grimpot interrupted eagerly.

"True so far as it goes," said the young captain. "But you may remember, Mr. Grimpot, having left me alone in your office one day when you called me in to discuss family affairs, and I happened to see a file on your desk I thought might be interesting. In it I found some very illuminating letters from my father to you, and you to my father. Very illuminating, indeed!"

The young captain paused, listening, as the doorbell rang in the hallway. Mr. Crawler started to hop from the room, but Jeremy put an arm out to stop him. "No need, Mr. Crawler," he said, "Mr. Cark will get it for you. I'm expecting some people to arrive."

And arrive they did moments later—eight burly seamen! The young captain immediately sent one to the back door of the dining hall, where he stood, an unsmiling sentry with brawny arms akimbo. In the meantime Mr. Trevelyan exchanged pointed glances with the three lawyers, who then made their way to the doorway leading to the front hall.

"We must return to our offices immediately," said Mr. Grimpot, giving the young captain a nervous smile. "We have some pressing business matters to attend to."

"I understand completely," said the captain, stepping aside to let the three go scurrying out, bumping into each other like three rubber balls in their frantic hurry to vanish from the room.

Mr. Cark then raised a questioning eyebrow at the captain, only to have him say, while making no attempt to lower his voice, "Let them go, Simon. They'll find outside their door my own legal counselor as well as several members of the Ladies' Aid and Good Works Society, which handsomely supports the Broggin Home for Boys. Thanks to the advice of Miss Dorcas here, they wish to take a close look at all records pertaining to the Home, as managed by Grimpot, Greazle, and Slypenny. My own legal counselor will, of course, be confiscating any papers he finds that are of interest particularly to me. Oh, and by the way, Mr. and Mrs. Crawler, do you keep any records we might find useful?"

"Oh no, indeed not," said Mrs. Crawler, her eyes darting nervously from side to side.

"No, none at all," added Mr. Crawler fervently.

At this, Colley tugged at Mr. Cark's coat sleeve, and then whispered something to him. Mr. Cark immediately ducked from the room.

"That is certainly too bad," said the young captain after a long pause. "I must say, though, I find this hard to believe."

"Well, it's true," said Mrs. Crawler indignantly. "And now we are being accused of lying as well as murder, with no proof of either."

She had, however, barely finished this speech when Mr. Cark ran back into the dining room and handed the captain a black notebook with a red spine. The Crawlers stared at him with frozen faces, motionless as a pair of lampposts as he thumbed through the book.

"Now isn't this interesting," he said. "Except for one boy, for whom for some reason you received payment, here is a record of what you paid out for each boy here. So it seems that you are in the business of buying boys, Mr. and Mrs. Crawler. Buying boys whom you then hire out to factories. And that, of course, Father, answers your earlier question of what connection you have with the Broggin Home for Boys. You are the owner of these factories! You can't deny that, can you?"

"No, I don't suppose I can," replied Mr. Trevelyan. Then he gave his son a long, hard, calculating look. "But would you like to tell me how you came by all this information? The factories, of course, you've always known about. That's no secret."

"How did I come by the rest of it?" said Jeremy. "Well, I owe a great deal to Simon Cark here, whom I've known for many years. He and I signed up together to go to sea as cabin boys aboard one of the ships belonging to Captain William Dorcas, who is here today accompanying his daughter, Belinda. But an accident, unfortunately, forced Simon to give up a life at sea and return to the land, although I continued at sea.

"Continued indeed! Went on to distinguish himself to such a degree that he is now in charge of his own ship!" Captain Dorcas explained, looking proudly at the young captain.

"Thank you for that, Captain Dorcas," said Jeremy. "But to go on, Simon Cark went into domestic service, writing me that he had found a place as head butler at the home of what he believed might be relatives of mine in the country. It was at Trevelyan House. Shortly after Mr. Grimpot informed me of Colley's ... ah ... death, Simon came to see me, telling me how almost all the staff had been let off. Later, when he returned to visit his friend Gampet, the head groomsman, he was told of Colley's disappearance. Gampet told him of a threat Colley made to run away. But Gampet thought that, as he put it, 'powerful little was done to find the lad,' in his opinion.

"Then when Miss Dorcas visited here for the first time with the Ladies' Aid and Good Works Society, she remarked how one young boy appeared to be unlike the others, who had come from less fortunate backgrounds. When she chanced upon him once more, she was able to learn from him that he had only come recently to the Broggin Home for Boys, and that he worked at the glass factory. I, of course, had no idea what Colley looked like, having last seen him when he was but an infant. Simon Cark came to my rescue by first making himself acquainted with Mr. Gorp, foreman at the glass factory, at the place where he ... ah ... refreshes himself after work. Simon provided Mr. Gorp with a liberal supply of his favored refreshments, and he, in turn, bragged to Simon of a boy from the Broggin Home, recently arrived, who would end up making him some money, if the young rogue would just show up again. 'Putting a stop to his breathing, if you know what I mean,' is how he put it to Simon.

"Finally, Simon stationed himself around the Broggin Home very nearly day and night to see if the boy was, in truth, Colley, and at last found him. And that, Father, is the story."

"Well," said Mr. Trevelyan, "it seems you have enough to make life very difficult for me, but I'd like to present my side of the story to you, Jeremy. However, I refuse to be airing dirty linen in front of an audience."

"It seems to me, Father," Jeremy replied, "that anyone willing to wear dirty linen should be willing to air it. But I agree that this is perhaps not the correct audience for it. See here, Captain Dorcas, would you be averse to taking six of our men here and all these boys down to the docks for a tour of one or two of your ships, and then perhaps treat them to a good feast afterward?"

"Why, I'd be honored to do that, Captain Trevelyan," replied Captain Dorcas, beaming.

"And would all you boys like that?" inquired the young captain.

All this time, of course, the boys had been sitting at the table with jaws hanging open, watching what was going on. Now they could not believe this invitation was actually being extended to them, and so they continued to sit and stare. Mrs. Crawler had something to say about it, however.

"The boys are not going anywhere, if you please," she snapped. "They are in the midst of their reading lessons, as you can see."

"Oh, is that so?" said the young captain smoothly. "Well, we'd certainly like to have a sample of their reading progress, if you don't mind. Miss Dorcas, who is the young man who read to you before? Perhaps he would like to show us what he has learned since you were last here."

Without waiting to learn whether Mrs. Crawler minded or not,

Miss Belinda Dorcas stepped lightly down the room, stopping behind where Marty sat.

"Would you like to read a little to us as you did before?" she asked, touching him gently on the shoulder.

Marty squirmed in his seat. Then squirmed again. "There were a rat an' a hole in the ground is where he's at. That's all there is 'bout that old rat," he recited in total misery.

"And what is the book he is . . . ah . . . *reading* from, Miss Dorcas?" asked Captain Trevelyan.

"It is one titled, *Building Techniques of the Sixteenth Century,*" replied Miss Dorcas.

"I see," said Captain Trevelyan. "Mr. and Mrs. Crawler, these boys are not in the midst of reading lessons. I don't believe they've had a reading lesson since they've been here, nor any other lessons. I don't believe half of them can even read. What I know is that these boys, rather than going to the glass factory or any other factory, are going to have a fine day climbing over ships in the fresh air. As for you two, one of my men will escort you to wherever it is that you live in this building, and there you will remain until the law takes over. If attempted murder cannot be proved, certainly child slavery can be. You should be put away for a very long time, and never be allowed to have anything to do with children again!"

Obadiah and Quintilla, eyes fixed straight ahead in a ghastly stare, were marched from the room under escort, without doubt never to be seen again by the boys of the Broggin Home.

"Lads," the young captain said in a commanding voice, "you must mind my men. I'm putting them in charge of you until tomorrow when I'm sure the ladies of the Ladies' Aid and Good Works Society will be making arrangements for the new Broggin Home for Boys, where you will be having proper lessons, training for your future, and kindly people looking after you. Now, you may throw those old books away, and be off with you!"

The boys at first did not seem to realize that all this good news applied to them. But as soon as one boy came to life and tried out the situation by throwing a book over his shoulder, the rest came to life as well. Soon books were flying about the room to the accompaniment of boys laughing and shouting and pushing each other. In truth, for the first time ever, the room sounded as if real boys were alive in it!

But Colley, standing beside his cousin, felt as if he had been forgotten. He tugged hesitantly on Jeremy's sleeve.

"What . . . what am *I* to do?" he asked.

Jeremy smiled down at him. "Why, you'll be going home, of course. Belinda, Mr. Cark, and I will be going with you, and we'll leave as soon as this is all over." He paused a moment, studying Colley's face. "But you look disappointed. Don't you wish to go, Colley?"

"Oh yes!" cried Colley. "But . . . but I would like my friends from here to go with me."

"I see," said Jeremy. "Well then, come along and tell Captain Dorcas who those friends are. When they're finished with their visit to the ships, he'll bring them right along to Trevelyan House. After all, we can't all fit in one cab, anyway."

As Colley was happily reciting the names of his friends to Captain Dorcas, the friends—Marty, Noah, Rufus, Toby, and Zack—all trooped out with the others. But all cast curious, side-long glances at Colley, almost as if they knew that he and they would now be in different worlds. They were gone before Colley had finished talking with Captain Dorcas.

"And," concluded Colley, "I should like an older boy named Soup to come as well, if it's all right."

"Of course it is, my boy!" said Captain Dorcas heartily. "And we shall all be meeting soon at Trevelyan House."

Then he too was gone.

"And now, Father," said Jeremy, "what is it you wanted to say to me?"

Chapter XXI

An Unacceptable Explanation

"I don't know whether or not what I have to say will make any difference to you, Jeremy," Mr. Trevelyan began, "but I must say it in any event.

"I believe you know that my mother, your true grandmother, died when I was a boy. My father, your grandfather, soon married again, and apparently loved his second wife a great deal more than his first. Perhaps because of that, or perhaps for some other reason, he ended having a great deal more love for their son than for the one from his first marriage. I tried not to notice it, but at the very least, I always supposed that, being the first and eldest son, I was to be the heir to the Trevelyan estate and most of the Trevelyan fortune.

"When my father died, he left all to his wife, my stepmother, with arrangements that when she died, the estate and the largest portion of the fortune was to go to their son, my half brother. I was able to suppress my anger, or at least try not to let it show.

"But I'm afraid that when my half brother and his wife produced this wizened baby, who grew into a frail, mollycoddled boy destined to inherit what should have been mine, while my own strapping, handsome son had run off, my anger could not be contained.

"I had often talked to Grimpot about this, but he informed me that nothing could be done about the will, and I would only inherit if the whole family died. Then he wrote me of my half brother and his wife's deaths while your stepmother and I were abroad, and presented a possible plan for removing their son from the picture. I thought it could not hurt the boy. Perhaps toughen him up a bit if nothing else. So I agreed to have him delivered to the Broggin Home."

"Father!" Jeremy burst out. "Are you still playing games with me? How can you expect me to believe such a lie? Or have you actually persuaded yourself to believe it? I remember your telling me this same sad lie as you took me around to your factories when I was growing up. I used to hate the sight of little boys no older than I was, begrimed, pitifully thin, with such heartbreakingly sad eyes. 'It's good for them to work here,' you told me. 'Toughens them up and prepares them for life.'

"But I knew inside me, even as a little boy, that you were lying. Those pitiful little fellows were grinding their lives away toward an early death. And all the while you kept telling me I was to follow in your footsteps and take over from you some day. I was too frightened to tell you I could never do that, and young enough to believe there was no way to escape but to run off. So I went to sea to find a better kind of life."

"Oh yes," said Mr. Trevelyan bitterly. "And of course you realize if I had inherited what should have been mine, I never would have even had to build my own fortune with factories. Had you ever thought about that?"

"Yes, Father," replied Jeremy. "But I remember asking you often, after being made miserable by what I saw, why you needed to employ these little boys. And do you remember what you always replied? 'I'm only doing it because of love for you, Son. And these boys earn less, so I can make more for you.' Oh, you wove a very tight net around me, Father.

"When you married Serena, I felt it would make no difference to speak out even if I dared, for you wanted to keep her in the lavish lifestyle she preferred. And as to the present, do you really believe I would want to become heir to the Trevelyan estate and fortune if I had any idea of what it took for me to have it? I cannot even imagine what drove you to such lengths, Father!"

"Well, and what do you now propose to do about all this?" asked Mr. Trevelyan, putting an arm around Serena Trevelyan, who had suddenly burst into tears. "What crimes do you intend to charge me with?"

"I don't know, Father," replied Jeremy. "It's all such a tangled web. Perhaps you can escape from all of it, and I probably won't pursue you. All I know is that I want none of what you have, for the sea is now my life. Belinda and I are to wed, and it is what she desires as well. All I hope is that at least you will give up the practice of allowing small, helpless young boys to work in your factories. Perhaps, if that occurs, you and I can some day come to terms with each other. But right now, I know of one young boy who would surely like to leave this place behind, and as quickly as possible. So come along, Colley.

"Father, I believe you and Serena can find your way out?"

Chapter XXII

A Very Acceptable
Invitation

As the wheels of the carriage began to roll, Colley looked out the window at the Broggin Home for Boys for what he hoped was the very last time. Still stunned and bewildered by all that had happened, he found it hard to believe he was leaving there finally and forever, sitting now in the cab across from his cousin Jeremy and Belinda Dorcas, and by the side of Simon Cark.

Simon Cark! *Cark!* Now known by Colley never to have been the owner of the rough voice heard only through a thick wool blanket. A voice, in truth, now known to bear no resemblance to Simon Cark's voice, but which Colley, in his terror, had attached to someone he believed, most mistakenly it now seemed, did not like him. Simon Cark, now known to be not the villain who stole Colley in the dead of night from Trevelyan House, but instead someone who *rescued* him from the clutches of the Broggin Home for Boys!

But all at once, this thought whirling through his head was interrupted by another, causing Colley to cry out when the carriage had traveled no more than a block or two.

"Oh! Please, Jeremy, we must stop and go back. Oh, please!"

"Why?" asked Jeremy, completely taken by surprise. "Don't tell me you wish to return to the Broggin Home, Colley."

"No, not there!" cried Colley. "I want to go to the graveyard. Oh, please, Jeremy!"

"Well, if that's what you wish, we'll return," said Jeremy, exchanging puzzled looks with Miss Dorcas. Then he leaned his head out the window and shouted to the driver to turn back.

When they arrived at the graveyard, Jeremy called to the driver to stop. Then he raced after Colley, who had started to scramble from the carriage almost before it stopped.

"You don't need to come with me!" Colley shouted over his shoulder.

"I'm coming anyway!" Jeremy shouted back. "I'm not letting you out of my sight."

He waited at the gate, however, as Colley flew to the far corner of the graveyard. There was the familiar box, but where was Abigail? Colley looked around the graveyard in despair. How was he to find the boys' pet amidst all those gravestones and tall weeds? Quickly, Colley began brushing aside the weeds, but there was no sign of Abigail. What if he had found an opening and waddled out of the graveyard, perhaps to be run over by a carriage? Had he even eaten the gummy bun Colley had left behind? Colley kneeled down to look into the box. The gummy bun was missing, but there in the far corner of the box lay Abigail, fast asleep! Gently, Colley tilted the box upright, put the cover back on, and lifted up the box.

Jeremy saw Colley struggling with the large box and instantly threaded his way among the gravestones to meet him.

"Here, let me help you," he said, taking the box away from Colley as if it weighed no more than a feather. "But might I ask what is in here that's so important?"

"It's Abigail," mumbled Colley.

"And who or what is Abigail?" asked Jeremy.

"He's . . . he's my friends' pet," replied Colley, sounding very defensive indeed.

"Well, I can see you just don't want to tell me," said Jeremy. "So I won't keep asking."

"All right then," Colley blurted. "Abigail is a rat, and I don't think Miss Dorcas would like it if she knew about it."

At which point, Jeremy burst out laughing. "Colley, Miss Dorcas is a true seaman's daughter who grew up knowing about rats. I don't believe she is in love with them, at least not in the quantities that sometimes infest her father's ships. But she told me that once as a small girl she thought about having one for a pet, for she had read about it in a magazine. So I don't believe you need have any fears on that score."

And, in truth, Miss Dorcas had a fit of giggles when she heard about a male rat with the name of Abigail, and that the name had been borrowed from a gravestone.

"And think how pleased the boys will be when they find their pet has been rescued," she said to Colley.

"I believe they will," he replied. "But is it true, Miss Dorcas, that you once wished for a pet rat?"

Miss Dorcas smiled. "Oh, I'm not quite sure that 'wished' is the correct word for it. I believe 'wondered about having' is more like it. But what I do wish is that you would call me Belinda instead of Miss Dorcas. After all, we are soon to be cousins, you know."

"I will!" Colley promised fervently.

"Well then, now that that's been settled to everyone's satisfaction," said Jeremy, "tell me, Colley, will you be sending Abigail back with the boys, or do you intend to keep him with you to be there whenever they come to visit?"

"V-v-visit?" stammered Colley. "But I thought they were coming to *live* with me!"

"Is that what you want?" Jeremy asked, giving Colley a searching look.

"They're my *friends!*" cried Colley. "They saved my life!"

"Saved your life!" exclaimed Jeremy. "But how? When?"

Colley drew a deep breath, for it was a long tale he had to tell. "It was when everyone thought I'd run away," he said. "Only I hadn't at all!"

He then went on to tell how he had become ill, and how the boys had hidden him in their secret den in the tunnel that led to the graveyard, and had nursed him back to health with unbelievable kindness and patience. Then he told how the tunnel was discovered by the Crawlers, with the trapdoor to it nailed shut. That was when he knew he had no choice but to run away. And that was when he was found by Mr. Cark.

"And to think all along we supposed you'd found a way to hide the whole time in the graveyard, and never thought to ask about it," Jeremy said, shaking his head in disbelief. "But I was so wrapped up in my concerns with my father, for it was after all a very difficult moment for me, that I could think of little else. But now I must say I understand why you think so much of these young friends of yours, and I'd like to hear much more about them."

"And so would I!" exclaimed Belinda.

So Colley went on to tell them more about the tunnel and the graveyard and how the boys had adopted families from names on the gravestones. But as he talked, his eyelids became heavier and heavier, and without even realizing that it was happening, he fell into a sound sleep, lulled by the sound of the rolling carriage wheels.

But oh, what he awoke to! For when they arrived at Trevelyan House, there on the front steps were Lucy and Jonas Winkle and Mrs. Whitley and Gampet, all awaiting the arrival of their young master with tears streaming from every eye. They had been alerted by a message sped to them the night before, one of many written by Captain Jeremy Trevelyan. Not knowing the exact time of arrival, they had all taken turns being posted at the front window, one by one. And then at last they had heard the sound of carriage wheels, and all raced pell-mell to the front door to greet him. There was so much hugging and petting and tears of joy shed, it was hardly to be believed!

But then it was Colley's turn to stand at a window, watching and waiting. He would not even allow Lucy to get him out of those "dreadful garments" and into "decent clothes." He did not want to look different from his friends when they arrived. And after all, what if Lucy were to insist he wear a ruffled shirt?

Late that afternoon, at long last, the wheels of a carriage were heard bowling down the driveway, and Colley ran to fetch Jeremy and Belinda to come with him to the front steps to meet it. But what a different meeting this was from the earlier one!

Captain Dorcas alighted from the carriage as cheerful as you please. But the boys, including Soup, all climbed out rubbing their eyes and looking bewildered, for they, like Colley, had fallen asleep in the carriage. The smile on Colley's face faded as they stood with blank faces, as if they were not certain they had ever seen him before.

Jeremy, however, quickly apprised the situation, and came to the rescue. "Colley," he said, "don't you have something you'd like to show your friends. You know what I mean, something out in the pantry."

"Oh yes, thank you, Jeremy!" Colley said eagerly. "Come along, everyone!"

So a solemn little parade of boys trailed after Colley through the immense entry hall, into a cavernous dining room, out into yet another hall, through a butler's pantry, into an enormous kitchen, and finally into a storage pantry. And it was there that Colley finally stopped and pointed to a box on the floor, a box very familiar to all present, except Soup.

"Sure an' ye ain't goin' to say as how that's Abigail's box?" Marty exclaimed.

"Open it and see," replied Colley.

As Marty lifted off the lid, the boys all crowded around, peering into the box.

"Well, if that ain't just it!" Toby said. "It's Abigail all right."

"Where'd you find him?" Zack asked. "We figgered as how he got buried in the tunnel."

"We was flippin' miserable," said Rufus.

"I knew you would be," Colley said. And then he went on to tell the tale of how he had been in the graveyard when the Crawlers discovered the tunnel and had gone back to rescue Abigail.

"Wheeoo!" breathed Noah. "Think how close he come to not bein' here. Wonder if he knows."

"Don't matter," Marty said. "He's here is what counts. Come on, Soup. Come see. Ye ain't never met Abigail."

Soup, who had been hanging back at the doorway to the pantry, then came shuffling over and peering into the box.

"Ye never knew we had him did ye, Soup?" Marty said.

Soup could only shake his head, too overwhelmed to speak.

"Ain't you goin' to tell Soup how we got Abigail?" Noah asked.

"If Soup don't mind waitin'," Marty said. "I'm dyin' to know wot them flippin' Crawlers was sayin' when they was in the tunnel and in the graveyard. Come on, tell us, Jed."

Minutes later, when Jeremy looked into the pantry, there the boys all were, seated cross-legged in a circle around Abigail's box, talking at full speed. Two of the boys had small scraps of paper in their hands, and one of them was waving it about excitedly.

"You got almost all the picter, Jed," he said. "An' it's just like them ships we was on today. Wish we could go back one day."

"Oh, I'm certain Jeremy will take you back, Noah," Colley said.

"I will, indeed, one day soon," Jeremy broke in. "But right now I believe there's something for you in the kitchen, so come along, all of you."

The boys speedily scrambled to their feet, and in no time were seated around a huge kitchen table laid with glasses, tall pitchers of lemonade, and great platters of cinnamon and raisin cookies. As all of them, including Colley, gulped down lemonade and stuffed cookies into their mouths, Mrs. Whitley and Lucy, who to their credit had never displayed so much as a look of surprise at these ragged little boys, stood with benign expressions watching the cookies disappear from the platters. Lucy, of course, could barely disguise a look of amazement at her charge busily stuffing one cookie after another into himself, almost without stop! It may be safely said that never before was there ever such a happy scene as this in the kitchen at Trevelyan House.

While this was going on, Jeremy, Belinda, Simon Cark, and Jonas Winkle had entered the kitchen and were quietly holding a meeting off in one corner. And they were there when Toby was heard to ask the table at large.

"How long do we get to stay here?"

"How . . . how long would you like to stay, Toby?" asked Colley.

"Oh, long as wot anybody would let me," replied Toby, licking cinnamon crumbs off his thumb. "Maybe even long as tomorrow."

Every boy's head very nearly nodded off its skinny neck at this idea. All except Soup, however, who had seemed almost paralyzed with shock at finding himself in such extraordinary surroundings ever since he stepped from the cab.

"I believe what Colley—whom you all seem to know as Jed— is really asking you," said Jeremy, stepping up to the head of the table, "is if you'd all like to come here to live?"

Nobody spoke. Nobody even moved. Like Soup, they all seemed to have become paralyzed, staring at Jeremy like so many statues in a park.

"Well?" inquired Jeremy. "Does no one have anything to say?"

"Faith an' do ye mean it?" asked Marty, finally coming to life.

"Of course we mean it," said Jeremy firmly.

Sudden wide grins broke out on all faces, except that belonging to Soup, and each grinning boy began punching his neighbor in the arm, the way they best knew to show how they felt.

"Soup, don't you wish to stay with the others?" asked Jeremy, who let nothing go unnoticed.

"I never thought as how you meant me," Soup said, his pale thin face reddening. "Wot would I do here with the others? I got more years than they do, so I ain't fit for lessons nor nothin' like that. An' all I ever done before I come to the Broggin Home was sweep up after horses on the streets. I never minded," he added with a faraway look in his eyes, "'cause I love bein' 'round horses."

"We could talk to Gampet, Captain," Mr. Cark broke in.

"Do you suppose you could go find him, Simon?" Jeremy asked.

"Right away!" said Mr. Cark.

And as it turned out, Gampet was right outside the back door, being loathe to miss out on what was transpiring in the kitchen. He came stumping in at once.

"Gampet, we have a young man here who claims he loves being around horses, and I expect would very much like to work with them," Jeremy said, pointing to Soup. "Can you use some help in the stables?"

"Oh, I can indeed, sir," replied Gampet. "All the rest got let go, and so it's just myself out there. I'm fair wore out."

"But . . . but I can't do work with horses," Soup faltered. "I got a bad leg and ain't fit for much." He stood up from the table and started across the floor, his one leg dragging.

Colley suddenly grinned. "Gampet, show him," he said.

Then Gampet lifted one side of his trousers to reveal—a wooden leg! "Come along, young fellow," he said cheerfully. "We'll get you started at once!"

The two went out the back door, the old man stumping along with his arm around the young man's shoulders. And it could well be said that there was no one happier in the whole world than that young man was just then!

"Now," Jeremy said, "before we go on with making plans,

there is something I am most curious about, and that is your all calling Colley 'Jed.' Do I take this to mean you were all given names not your own?"

The boys all nodded.

"My name were John," Zack said.

"My name were Timothy," said Noah.

"My name were Edward," said Toby.

"My name were Luke," said Rufus.

"An' my name were Marty," said Marty.

"Wot do you mean, yer name were Marty?" asked Zack. "You bein' funny or somethin'?"

"No," replied Marty, grinning. "Them Crawlers went and give me me own name. Me tears was flowin' for them two, makin' such a mistake. But faith, wot were I to do?"

It took some minutes before the grinning and punching in the ribs over this settled back down.

"Well, as that is all explained," Jeremy said, "now I'll explain how everything is to be here. Mr. Cark has agreed to return as head butler, which is to say, he's in charge, and you're all to mind him. That's all right with you, isn't it, Colley?"

"Oh yes!" said Colley wholeheartedly.

Lucy, standing nearby, beamed upon hearing this. She, of course, having now been apprised of Simon Cark's part in rescuing Colley, could not possibly ever have anything but the warmest feelings toward him.

"Lucy," continued Jeremy, "will have charge of seeing to it that all of you boys get to bed on time, rise on time, keep clean, and are properly clothed."

"As for that, Mr. Jeremy," said Lucy, "I will have Mrs. Ramkin up from the village tomorrow, and she shall start sewing for the boys at once. In the meantime, I think some of Colley's clothes will serve quite well. And for the present, Colley certainly has enough nightshirts to go around, I'm thankful to say."

At this, Colley felt the blood drain from his face. "Oh no, Lucy, they can't wear my nightshirts!"

"Why ever not, Master Colley?" Lucy asked.

"They . . . they . . . all have ruffles!" he blurted.

"And what's wrong with ruffles?" asked Lucy indignantly.

"I . . . I . . . I don't . . . I . . . I . . . can't . . . I . . ." faltered Colley, breaking down completely in confusion and misery.

Marty now looked hard at the former Noah, and when Noah nodded, he looked at the former Zack. As soon as Zack nodded, he looked at the former Rufus and former Toby, who both did the same.

"See here, Jed," Marty said, clearly not quite ready for the name 'Colley,' "we all done took a vote, an' if yer Lucy says we're to wear ruffles, we'll wear them ruffles. So no more said 'bout it. Cap'n, ye got any more to tell us?"

"Why yes, Marty, I do," replied Jeremy. "I shall arrange to be appointed Colley's guardian, and when I have to go to sea, Mrs. Trevelyan, the present Miss Belinda Dorcas, shall speak for me. If any of you have any problems, you're to come to us. And now last, but far from the least, you will all be having school lessons, and Mr. Jonas Winkle will be in charge of that."

"Will we be learnin' to read?" asked Marty. "Some o' us ain't never learned how."

"I'll see that you do learn," promised Jonas Winkle. "But as none of you has ever really gone to school, I must warn you, it will be hard work."

"Sure an' it's wot we want," said Marty. "Ye ain't goin' to hear any o' us complainin'."

"And, Jonas," Colley announced solemnly, "I must tell you that . . . that's the . . . the flippin' truth, because . . . because Marty don't tell lies!"

While the boys all produced cheerful grins upon hearing this, Jonas Winkle, to *his* everlasting credit, never so much as blinked an eye!

: